Thomas Seaton Donoho

Ivywall

Thomas Seaton Donoho

Ivywall

ISBN/EAN: 9783337047566

Printed in Europe, USA, Canada, Australia, Japan

Cover: Foto ©Andreas Hilbeck / pixelio.de

More available books at **www.hansebooks.com**

BY

T. SEATON DONOHO,

AUTHOR OF "MOENA," &c.

WASHINGTON, D. C.:

THOMAS McGILL, PUBLISHER.

1860.

"And this our life, exempt from public haunt,
Finds tongues in trees, books in the running brooks,
Sermons in stones, and good in everything."

SHAKSPEARE.

IVYWALL.

TO MY FRIEND,

JOHN SAVAGE,

HISTORIAN, DRAMATIST, AND POET,

"WHOSE HEART AND BRAIN WITH LOVE AND GENIUS GLOW,"

"IVYWALL"

Is Affectionately Dedicated.

IVYWALL.

Ivywall.

THE hours at Ivywall pass pleasantly,
Beneath the maple and the willow shade,
Or in the latticed bower of morning-glories,
Whose purple beakers catch the dew all night,
Till Dawn, intruding on the revelry,
Drinks in hot haste the few remaining drops.

Pleasantly pass the hours at Ivywall,
On the far-seeing belvedere : the city
Pictured below me, and the waving plains,
And the blue circle of the white-sailed river,
That, hearing ocean's call, from hill to hill
Runs eagerly, to find a portal there,
Seeming, at last, to vanish in the sky,
And so to seek its love : even as the soul,
That grows impatient of the bonds of earth,
And leaves the long-accustomed track of time,
Obedient to the voice, Eternity !

Pleasantly pass the hours at Ivywall,
On the grape-clambered balcony, where reach
The maple boughs, that rock the nested birds,

And all the little leaves clap hands together,
Applauding, while the parent of the brood
Sits by her young, and sings so tenderly!

The hours at Ivywall pass pleasantly,
Reclining on the checkered grass, beside
The circle, rainbow-like, of many flowers,
Whose centre is an everblooming rose.
And even as this many-colored round,
So is my life at Ivywall: replete
With beauty and enjoyment.　And the rose,
That is its central ornament and pride—
Thou art the Rose, dear Maye, my Sweetheart-Wife!

Pleasantly pass the hours at Ivywall,
With friends, who have not studied books alone,
Though much of those, but varied nature, too,
And all the harmonies.　And still the chief,
By birthright and the claim of sympathy,
My Brother, whom in early years I taught
My own small knowledge of attunéd words,
By him so soon acquired, so fast improved,
So wedded to the music of his soul,
And with such melody of voice expressed,
That he has paid me back a thousand fold.
And oft at sunset, oft beneath the moon,
His song hath linked all hearts in happiness;
And dearer for his sake is Ivywall!

In spring, while watching bud by bud unfold;
In summer, resting in the breezy shade;
In autumn, when the red and yellow leaves

Come fluttering down to strew my winding walks;
In winter, when the dial, capped with snow,
No longer tells of time's mysterious flight—
Pleasantly pass the hours at Ivywall!

Then in my little book-room glows the grate;
Then is my Love more fondly by my side,
For all the bitter winds that moan without;
Then is my Brother's song more musical,
That every icy tree is voiceless;
Then is my Friend, my next-to-brother, welcome;*
And changeful converse then, and chosen books,
Make bright the darkest day; and day to night
Steals silently, unnoticed, and again
Almost the night to morning.

     Or, alone,
The nature-tracing pencil gives me scenes
That glow with summer grandeur; or the pen
Paints from the heart a gallery for hearts,
Wherein no picture may be excellent,
Yet each, I fondly fancy, hath a touch
Of heart-glow that may make it dear to some—
Recalling memory in her fairest looks,
Giving new sunshine to the present day,
And confidence to meet the veiléd future.

Thus, beauty blooming round me, hope alluring;
Thus, blessed with peace and love, and friends and
   books,
And such affection for the good and grand,

* JOHN SAVAGE.

Their inspiration from my soul is cast—
Ah, that it must be faintly!—on the page,
And many-tinted canvas; thus, possessed—
And this my bolder claim!—of deep desire
That of my life's enjoyments I may form
Enjoyment, as a crown, for other lives—
Pleasantly pass the hours at Ivywall!

The Bird of the Lamp.

In a morning walk through the Capitol Garden, I observed a bird in one of
the gas-lamps—strange prison-place!—where it was fluttering against the glass,
striving to escape.

Poor little Captive! thou whose joy till now
  Was change, and sweeter change, from tree to tree,
Or, falling like a blossom from the bough,
  To dart among the vines where sips the bee,
  Or trip along the grass, or warble free
Thy love-song from some high and swaying limb,
Or pour the notes of morn or even hymn:

Poor little Captive! weary, broken-hearted,
  Lone in thy crystal prison-house, to look
Forth on the May-Day world, from which thou 'rt parted
  Even as with iron bars! And lo! the brook
  Leaping before thee, through the dear green nook
Of happy summers, where—O cruel fate!
Perchance thou hearest now thy calling mate!

Calling and calling, evermore in vain,
   Despairing in the bowers where once was peace,
While all her sisters, hearing her complain,
   Throng round her desolate home, and still increase
   The mournful melody which may not cease!
Poor bird, thy failing voice in love replying,
Prisoner in sight of liberty, and dying!

No! thou art free! I give thee to the breeze,
   That greets thy rapid flight with sweets of May;
I give thee to the tall and beckoning trees,
   That were less joyous when thou wert away:
   I give thee back to all the beauteous day!
Back to the earth below, the sky above—
To life, and liberty, and joy, and love!

True to the nature of all minstrelsy,
   Thou ownest love is life's divinest boon,
Seeking at once thy mate, and leaving me
   Even unthanked! But mayst thou find her soon,
   And when your mutual joy hath highest noon,
Unscared by clouds—then shall I be repaid,
Listening your music down the odorous glade!

And I have longings, too, dear bird, like thine—
   Longings for life, and liberty, and love!
Here, in a world-wide prison, here I pine,
   Forthgazing at my own blest home—above!'
   Where blooms the beautiful, immortal grove—
Where flow the living streams, where angels sing,
And friends I loved and lost are beckoning!

E'en now the glory from that land of light
   Pierces my prison walls; but when I seek,
Lured by its brilliancy, to wing my flight,
   Alas, the world is strong and I am weak!
   But soon, full well I know, a FRIEND will speak,
Kindly, the word of power, and I shall rise
Free from the earth and welcome to the skies!

Book Song.

NIGHT—and alone: yet not alone,
   For round me are my books—
A thousand friends! so fondly known!
     So all my own!
   What friends are like my books!

I know that in these iron times,
   And in this Labor Land,
To love the Muse is worst of crimes—
     And yet, sweet Rhymes!
   I dare to love ye still!

Therefore around my pictured room
   In all her graceful forms appears
Bright Poesie! Her Heaven-caught bloom,
     In joy or gloom,
   Dear to my soul, and blest!

What concerts of angelic kind
  Within these narrow walls are heard,
When Milton—and the Mighty Mind,
      The Unconfined,
The Bard of Avon, sing!

When, ever and anon, the voice
  Of many another Bard glides in;
And I, luxurious, have my choice,
      To weep—rejoice—
Be gay or sad at will!

I number not among my friends,
  My book-friends, one of those
Who in Religion's name *contends*,
      And fiercely bends
The controversial bow!

Leave me alone to love and song,
  For love is wise, and song is good!
My guardians have they been from wrong,
      And will, ere long,
Welcome me home, to GOD!

Nor have I, 'mid my thousand, one
  Who talks to me of party strife.
Such slanderous wars—who win—who run—
      I care for none:
Leave me to pensive Peace!

Soul-Song.

THOU hast gone to the Home of the Highest,
  Through the beautiful gates of the stars!
Thy wings are like snow, and thou fliest,
  Exulting, set free from thy bars,
And the world is beneath thee forever,
  And past are its shadows and fears :—
But wilt thou forget us?   Ah, never!
  Nor leave us, unloved, in our tears!

For the spirits of dear-ones departed
  Look down from the region of love,
With a smile so sincere and warm-hearted
  That it kindles the seraphs above;
It glows 'mid the ranks of the Holy,
  Its sympathy circles the sky,
And, raised by its glory, the lowly
  With angel-like rapture reply!

The world in its grandeur is only
  The footstool of HIM on the Throne;
We wander the world, and are lonely,
  And the day and the night hears our moan;
But GOD, and the good whom HE taketh,
  With tenderness see us and aid,
And we die, and our true life awaketh,
  "Where no one shall make us afraid!"

Scene of the Olden Days.

It was the changeful April time,
  The time of sun and showers,
And the timid leaves, they were peeping forth,
  And the delicate-tinted flowers.

Glowing and balmy the day had been,
  Like a day of summer's pride,
And its beauty conquered every heart,
  Like the presence of a bride.

Night stole upon the landscape now,
  Serene and starry night;
Soon would the moon come over the hill,
  Where shone her herald, Light.

Two grey, fantastic clouds appeared,
  Two clouds like living things,
Gigantic vultures of the Alps,
  Meeting with outstretched wings.

"I fear it!" a trembling maiden spoke,
  And lowered her large, dark eyes.
"Fear not!   'Tis only the sultry day,"
  A manly voice replies.

"Not that! not that!" said the maiden fair,
  "No tempest would I fear,

But to leave the home I have loved so long,
    But to leave my father dear!"

" O, father! father! can I forget
    How kind thou hast been to me!
Shall a daughter leave thy feeble age
    To a stern world's mockery!"

" Be calm!   Thy tears are burning tears,
    They burn into my heart!"
He caught that small and fevered hand,
    But still would the hot tears start.

" Be calm! I love thee with all my soul!
    I know thou lovest again!
'Tis a vow in Heaven!   What power of earth
    Shall ever unbind the chain!

" Not with cruelty speak I now,
    But to-night thy choice must be:
A father's command—or a lover's vow!
    Reflect, and answer me!"

There was a struggle of many thoughts
    In the maiden's troubled breast:—
She cast herself in her lover's arms,
    And thus was her choice confest!

He hath placed the young girl's drooping form
    On the back of an eager steed;
His lordly stride another feels—
    And away with breathless speed!

Away, the bounding steeds, away!
   Through the wood, and by the sea!
Once only the maiden looks behind,
   With a wild look, tearfully!

It is the tower, the tower of home,
   It is the taper's light,
Where her father bends o'er the learnéd page,
   So far into the night.

And over the tall, dark tower appear
   Two clouds, like living things:
Alas, no more an idle dream
   Are now those vulture wings!

But away! away! "Be calm, my love!
   To-morrow shall all be well!"
Her lover's words came sad to her
   As the sound of a midnight knell!

"Thy father shall we see again,
   We shall know his forgiving smile!"
She cast her eyes to Heaven, to pray :—
   The clouds grew dark the while.

Darker and darker grew the clouds,
   More strange and vast their form;
The lightning flashed to light the path
   Where heavily rolled the storm.

What hurrying tramp on the winding shore?
   Ha! see by the lurid glare—

The long, white beard, and the streaming locks—
    The old man riding there!

Riding there, at the head of his troop,
    To claim his faithless child.
A broad, bright flash of the lightning wrath,
    And their own as sudden and wild!

By the father's arm the lover falls,
    Dead on the desert shore:
"Traitor! Receive thy recompense!"
    And the deed of blood was o'er.

Sprang away the masterless horse,
    Stood all the troop aghast:
The old man turned—O, GOD! how soon
    His avenging passion past!

For rider and steed—his own fair child—
    Dead—dead by the lightning stroke!
And over her pallid face he bent—
    He bent—no word he spoke.

Softly he touched her pallid cheek,
    Gently he raised her head.
His men did tremble all with fear,
    When he laughed above the dead!

" Ha, ha! ha, ha!" he laughed aloud:
    " Sir Bard, an epitaph!
An old fool's daughter! Ha! ha! ha!"—
    It was a maniac's laugh!

May Morning.

This morning, from my city home,
  Over the green fields straying,
I met, all robed in dresses white,
  The merry maidens Maying:

The merry maidens Maying,
  And a beau for every belle,
Who, like a knight of the olden time,
  Did guard his treasure well.

Their voices mingled sweetly,
  And their artless laughter rose,
And life to them seemed a sunny May,
  That would never, never close!

Each proudly bore the prize of flowers,
  Still adorned with diamond dew.
Lovely and glad was all to see,
  For the world to all was new.

And I felt the influence beaming
  Pleasantly over my heart,
And in all their joy and dreaming
  I took a willing part.

Returning again to childhood,
  And the happiness of May,
And the maiden, with golden tresses,
  My sweetheart all the way.

And the group beneath the blossoming trees,
  And the crowning of the Queen,
And the feast, and dance, and the lightsome song
  That ever would rise between.

I felt no longer old,
  In the memory of those hours,
And I stooped and gathered a handful
  Of little starry flowers.

Fanny.

Again the bright and pleasant days
  Are coming!   Look around!
The brook in joyous freedom strays,
  With its old, familiar sound!

The flowers that loved the sparkling brook
  Will hear its jubilant call,
And one by one from the margin look,
  Nodding their gay heads all!

And trees will arch their boughs above,
    And the sunbeams, here and there,
Will pierce the shade, as the light of love
    Visiting dark despair!

And hills and dales once more assume
    Their many-tinted green,
And birds, amid the wildering bloom,
    Make fairy-land the scene!

But dearer than ever, a thousand times dear,
To me will the beauty of Spring-time appear,
For Fanny—who drooped in the fierce winter hours—
Hath Spring-time again, and will bloom with the flowers!

She will rise, she will live, and her presence impart
The warmth of the May to my winter-cold heart,
As she moves like an angel, whose soft-spreading wings
Bear sweetness and pleasure, surpassing the Spring's!

Eras of Early Life.

BEAUTIFUL Fanny, when I saw thee first,
Thy bloom was that of some sweet rose-bud, nurst
With tenderness, beneath a foreign sky,
Unfolding timidly its charms; and I
Gazed on that rare and delicate surprise,
And loved thee, even while within my eyes
The tear of pity came.   These mingled feelings
Were caused by fancy's bright and dark revealings;
My love was like a day of happiness,
My fear was like a cloud, that told distress
Advancing swiftly, soon, perchance, to shade
All the dear light thy dawning beauty made.
I loved thee, not alone because thy face
And slender form possessed unusual grace,
But also, and the more, because I found
A spirit there that never would be bound
By the cold world's decrees, but freely live,
And gladly through its course its magic give
Of innocent joy, to make each sighing breast
A temple for that Heaven-descended guest.
And then I feared for thee, I pitied thee,
Lest wrong and sharp deceit should presently
From cruel hearts assail.   So true wert thou,
So unsuspecting was thy placid brow.

I have learned better since.   The GOD who gave
Thy spirit's artlessness, was strong to save.

'Twas May-Day eve.   Among the forest trees
Came wildly wandering forth the pleasant breeze,
And slanting fell the sunset rays of gold,
And down the rocky hill the streamlet rolled,
With ringing laugh of music.   And again,
And still at intervals, the sweet, shrill strain
Of birds came by.   But now a sweeter song
Uprose.   It was a young and white-robed throng
Of happy girls who sang, presenting one
A crown of flowers.   The coronation done,
And thou the Queen, dear Fanny! every eye
Grew brighter, welcoming thy kind reply.
Then songs and dances made a fairy scene,
And ne'er so glad a court, so loved a Queen!
No envy there; each pretty, blushing Miss
Came forward with her offering—a kiss,
Each owned thee fairest, every heart sincere
Confessed thee dearest still, where all were dear!

Thus ended May-Day, and it was the last
With school and school-companions. Spring-time passed,
And summer, bringing beauty to the earth,
Brought brighter charms to thee, more gentle mirth,
But still-increasing pleasure, though, alone,
Pensive, or reading, hour and hour hath flown,
Still wert thou happy then, and more than ever,
Thy mind expanding, with its proud endeavor
To clasp the infinite, in truth and love,
All good the world contains, and wisdom, peace, above!

Yet other seasons saw thee seeming sad,
No charm the book, the song, the pencil, had,
3

To win thy brightness back.   If friends appeared,
No more their merry words, their laughter cheered.
But hark ! a well-known step is on the street,
And—Fanny ! Fanny !

                    But when lovers meet
Let no eye see, no listening ear attend,
Let every tongue its silly babbling end !
Those times were sacred.   Even the poet will,
For once—it is a mighty task !—be still !

Time flies—but not to lovers, when apart :
Love's dial, marked upon a lover's heart,
How slow its shade, again how swiftly, moves !
Wouldst know time's progress ?   Ask not one who loves !

And yet the summer's pride, the winter's gloom
Departed, and the spring began to bloom,
And May-Day came once more, and on that Day
Stood Fanny, blushing in a bride's array,
And words were spoken that embraced a life :
A glad young lover claimed a loving wife.
How looked their trustful souls through future time !
What pictures formed they of a joy sublime !
The world was love, there was no world beside !
Beautiful world ! where GOD HIMSELF is guide !

And time passed on.   Their hearts were truly one,
And those its gentle beauty beamed upon,
Received the light with smiling.   Tearful eyes
Looked up with gratitude and sweet surprise,

And blest them.   And along their peaceful way
The sun was ever bright, the flowers were ever gay!

And time passed on.   Once more the spring was green.
And where was Fanny?

                    There! Her face serene,
But pale—so pale!   The joy of love is fled:
One silent stands, bending above the dead,
Mournfully, mournfully!   The dead are two—
A child, whose moments here were only few,
As if a cherub came to call the wife,
Then both departed to the Better Life!

The Heart's Memory.

I WROTE a song, a sweet-toned song,
   Of love, when I was young.
It was, mayhap, a silly strain—
   I care not—Ella sung!
And from its gentle melody
   The bliss of Eden sprung!

I wrote of deep philosophy—
   The world, approving, read.
I smiled, but even as I smiled
   The transient pleasure fled:
I thought upon an old-time song—
   I thought of Ella—dead!

I wrote to-day a single verse,
  First written long ago,
Once sung by her whose form the earth
  Never again may know :
It soon shall be my epitaph,
  The cypress shade below.

Love Vale.

They tell me I am old :
  In the dreary Winter, well, 'tis so ;
But when I walk the hills of Spring,
  My glad heart answers : "No !"

The pale green, peeping grass,
  The little star-like flowers,
The brook just free, the blossoming tree—
  Ah, they give me back young hours !

And down in the shadowed vale,
  Where the beautiful willows wave,
Sweet trysting-place of my timid love—
  Of my love who is in her grave !

Not there—not there ! I must not go there ;
  For the vale of my young delight,
'Tis a lonesome place, and its shadows fall
  On my heart like a haunted night.

I, that loved her so well,
  I—poor, dreaming boy!—
That dreamed a dream of Heaven on earth—
  Alas, for earthly joy!

Not there—not there! I must not go there,
  But over the hills away,
For the Spring is abroad, like an angel of peace,
  And her summons I obey.

Spring, she is sent from Heaven,
  Not only to gladden the earth,
But repeat to the soul, and still to repeat,
  The boon of its second birth.

And whatever cares I have known,
  And whatever ills surround,
They sink like the snow—and beauty leaps
  From the lately frozen ground.

In the sunny air, in the soothing breeze,
  I am no longer old,
Anew in my heart blooms the rose of love,
  In my heart but now so cold.

And down to the vale I may go again,
  Where the trysting willows wave,
And may talk with her whom I may not see,
  With my love beyond the grave!

3*

The Telegraph of Mind.

O, the thoughts that voyage ever,
  Silent, viewless, through the air!
Thoughts of fond-ones, sad-ones parted,
  Thoughts like angels, white and fair!
Day and night, day, night, forever,
  Round the earth, nor there confined;
Earth and Heaven in spirit union
  By the Telegraph of Mind!

Ye busy crowds, from morn to even,
  Toiling through the narrow street,
Your souls intent on golden treasure,
  Gold alone to you is sweet!—
Nay, not so: in all the many
  Shall ye look in vain for one
Whose thoughts launch not upon this voyage,
  Still beginning, never done!

For those we all have, dear unto us,
  By the ties of nature dear,
By the sympathy of friendship,
  By the charm of smile and tear,
Loved-ones, now by seas divided,
  Now by mountains dark and grand,
Or by that unmeasured ocean
  Rolling to the Spirit Land!

I gaze upon the beaming morning,
  And I bless it, for I know,
Up, forever, through its glory,
  How such fond Thoughts go!
I gaze upon the softening evening:
  Tireless Thoughts, ye still are there!
And eagerly my own thoughts join ye,
  Strong and glad with prayer!

Then I gaze on Men, my brothers;
  O, my soul is fonder then!
For these love-thoughts, fellow-travelers,
  Teach me how divine are men!
Yes, divine, despite all preaching,
  Though in some things wrong and blind;
For Earth and Heaven are still in union
  By the Telegraph of Mind!

The Stranger.

THOU little stranger from the Spirit Land,
  Welcome to Earth! Thou comest to us now
To take the pilgrim staff, at GOD's command,
  And join our long procession. Even as thou,
So came the INFANT, in the olden time,
And walked the world, and rendered life sublime.

The path HE trod is offered now to thee;
　Walk thou therein : it is the path of peace.
Remembering HIM, thy pilgrimage shall be
　Bordered with pleasantness, until it cease,
And radiant angels, waiting at the end,
Shall bear thee, joyous, to thy heavenly FRIEND!

Welcome to Earth!　Welcome, again, to Earth!
　Call we thee "Stranger?"　Ah, thou art not so,
For loving hearts were happy at thy birth,
　Ready with thee along thy path to go,
Pledging to HIM, who gave thee from above,
Guidance and guard, with constant prayer and love!

"GOD is a jealous GOD."　Forget not, then,
　Your vow to guide aright HIS trusted child.
Teach him to love and be beloved of men,
　Teach, if he sin, how sin is reconciled.
A soul is now your charge!　Be kind and wise,
Truly to train it for its native skies!

Child of my friends, though life to thee is yet
　Scarcely reality—a half-wake dream—
A day may come—when my day may be set—
　Perchance thy wondering eyes on this may beam.
Then, wouldst thou know who wrote thee thus—'tis one
Who for the parents' sake did love their son.

My fame is little now, and may ere long
　Be nothing : love is more to me than fame,
So I would be remembered in my song
　More by sincerity than other claim :

My heart speaks here, though all it cannot speak :
Strong hearts in love find ever words are weak.

Welcome, once more, and then, awhile, farewell,
    STANLEY !   A warrior's name in ancient story !
But he from whom thou hast it—proud to tell !—
    Hath found a brighter way to deathless glory—
The flower-strewn way of Art !   Learn, boy, as he,
Virtue, in Beauty's path, with joy to see !

And ere thou see her, wouldst thou know how fair,
    How fond, how faithful, all-beloved she is,
Look on thy mother's face, and learn it there ;
    And while thy look brings down thy mother's kiss,
O, learn that Virtue's smile is like thy mother's,
And, winning one, thou 'rt certain of the other's !

Lillie.

THOU art gone, and we mourn thee as one
Whose pilgrimage, only begun,
With beauty and gladness attended,
And a promise of happy years—ended !

Thy life was a May-Day of flowers,
And its light and its sweetness were ours,
For even an angel could be
But equal in fondness to thee!

So like to the angels wert thou,
Who art of their company now,
That we should not look round with surprise,
That we should look alone to the skies!

So like to the angels: we saw
Thy loveliness even with awe,
And felt in thy presence the charm
To shield us and save us from harm.

For this didst thou come to the earth,
The secret was this of thy birth.
Thou hast taught us the beauty of love,
Thou hast gone to its triumph above!

For this didst thou go to the skies,
And also to teach us to rise:
We follow: still show us the way;
And pray for us, Child-Angel, pray!

"Mattie."

So dearly loved, so worthy love,
So fair, and lost so soon!
So beautiful with hope thy Spring,
Thy Summer—ere its noon,
Gone—gone forever!

These flowers—and with how sweet a smile !—
　　Thou gavest unto me ;
In loveliness they still live on—
　　But Death hath come to thee—
　　　　　Rose of home's Eden !

Yet even Death, so often harsh,
　　Death, even, learned to smile :
Thine eyes were like an angel's eyes—
　　They touched his heart, the while
　　　　　His hand descended !

Thou didst not see him : he had sent
　　A vision on before,
Which hid his coming : 'twas a view
　　Of GOD's eternal shore—
　　　　　Glad angels waiting !

Thy soul with answering gladness spoke :
" O, garden ! heavenly fair !
Beautiful flowers !"　Silence then—
　　Then only Death was there !
　　　　　She with the vision !

Now bring ye flowers, ye white-robed girls,
　　Bring flowers of sweetest bloom—
Dear were ye both to her !—bring flowers,
　　And strew them o'er her tomb,
　　　　　Fondly, O, fondly !

To an Unknown Lady.

My friend has told me that he loves,
    Though whom—I do not know,
Save only, she has power to bid
    His heart's deep fountain flow.

And this for me is proof enough
    That she is worthy love,
That she alone has peace for him,
    His olive-bearing dove!

Therefore with him do I rejoice,
    Therefore with him unite
In gratitude to Heaven and you,
    Since thus are all things right.

'Tis right that he should choose so well,
    And you should grant his choice;
'Tis right that Truth with Love should dwell,
    And friend with friend rejoice.

Here, on the altar of your hearts,
    I breathe a reverent vow:
May HE, whose sweetest name is " Love,"
    Guide and protect you now !

Guide and protect you, day by day,
  Till all life's days be done,
And bless you with a welcome smile
  Where love and Heaven are one !

Soul unto Soul.

SOMETIMES, in this eventful pilgrimage,
Whose rest is in the land we know not of,
Across our path a lovely spirit comes,
Speaks a few words of grace and majesty,
Or cheers and charms us with a look, a smile,
Then leaves us in a dream; wherein we walk,
Year after year—still in that pleasant dream.
Soul haunteth soul: abroad throughout the world
Fond sympathy is seeking sympathy:
Spirits that GOD created like, seek like—
Found seldom, seldom even when found retained,
Though purest joy attends the recognition;
And love illimitable, peace and power,
Not for themselves alone, but all who need,
Seem promised by the moment's interview—
Yet strangely baffled : Why? Go ask of Heaven!

It may be, 'mid the doubts and wild alarms
That rise around us wheresoe'er we go,
'Twere time unfit for such sublime communing;

It may be, we should droop with doubts and fears,
If unsupported by such visitants,
And, having such forever, be too blest,
Nor further seek the Promised Land of GOD.

Pilgrim, go on, rejoicing!   When thou seest
One whom thou wouldst have known, and must have loved,
Suddenly leave thee—still, go on, rejoicing!
Many the paths conducting to the " Rest,"
Where all shall meet at last in full delight,
And spirit to its kindred spirit spring,
Most intimate, assured!

O, brothers! brothers!
How do I long to clasp ye to my heart,
And find, though never we embraced before,
Congenial love and longing throbbing there!

〜〜〜〜〜〜〜

In Memory.

In the swift circle of one little year,
  Maiden, and wife, and mother!
  Sweet changes—but another
Leaves thee, lamented, here!
Best joy and darkest grief in that short space:
  Yet now, above us,
  Ever to guard, and ever love us,
Last change of all—hast thou an angel place!

Charms.

I saw thee smile!—
   As purely bright
   As the dewy light
Of the odorous summer morn!

I heard thee speak!—
   And words like those
   The lily and rose
Of Eden bent to hear!

Thy voice in song!—
   All joys of love,
   All bliss above,
Came to my raptured soul!

"Sweet Sixteen."

THE coming on of summer time—
   The growing dawn of day—
The progress doth surpass the prime,
   Whatéver old-beards say!
From birth to death shall nought be seen
So beautiful as "Sweet Sixteen!"

See yonder Sage, before whose word
  We bend in reverence down—
But Beauty! when her voice is heard,
  Rebellion strikes the crown!
Easy to choose it is, I ween:
The Lord of Mind—or "Sweet Sixteen!"

Ah me! the bud becomes a flower,
  Matures and fades amain!
Pale Beauty! where is now thy power?
  Thy wintry smile is vain!
Not so: the heart, the heart is Queen,
Bright and eternal "Sweet Sixteen!"

Love and the Willow.

Like the willow-tree true love is;
When the battling storm above is,
Storm may bend, but may not break it,
Gentleness will ne'er forsake it,
Strength and gentleness together
Arm it 'gainst the wildest weather.
First in Spring its grace appeareth,
Last of all, its beauty cheereth!

Our Home.

Thou only Land of Liberty!
  Thou only Star amid the night!
Pale Nations, wondering, look to thee:
  Their hearts beat fast, their eyes grow bright!

When first thy Heaven-lit banner rose,
  It waved above the forest wild—
The world's proud chivalry thy foes:
  And yet thy stormy morning smiled!

The cause of Truth, O Native Land!
  The sacred cause of Truth was thine;
To God was raised thy arméd hand:
  And lo! a wonder and a sign!

A wonder, such as never Earth
  In all her revolutions gave—
The New-World Hercules, whose birth
  The tyrant awed, and roused the brave.

A sign, that while the stars shall burn,
  That while the rainbow spans the sky,
The flood of wrong shall not return,
  The fires of Freedom shall not die!

4*

The Day by Potomac.

When I may wander—but with thee no more—
Along Potomac's leafy, rocky shore:
There the calm water, where the glowing sky,
With softer tints reflected, charms the eye:
There all the glorious ranks of terraced trees,
Bright with the sunset, vocal with the breeze:
There, mossy rock, brook-lighted vale, sweet flowers:
All—all will whisper me of happy hours,
As by Potomac's memory-haunted shore
Slowly I wander—but with thee no more!

The gentle hills to sister hills inclining:
The solitary groves: the gay vines twining:
The separate trees: or two or three, which raise
Their lovelier arms, commanding loftier praise:
'Twas not, 'twas not in vain such fond appeal:
Quick was thine eye to see, thy heart to feel;
And, with the poet's, with the artist's thought,
Thou gavest to Nature all the praise she sought,
Who, therewith proud, whene'er thy sweet words fell,
Waved thee a thousand blessings,—and—farewell!

When I may wander—but with thee no more—
The wild, wild paths along Potomac's shore:
Many the voices that shall come to me,
Many the graceful forms shall picture thee!

Bird, breeze, and brook have caught thy tone for aye:
The waterfall, that in its careless play
Leaps down the rocks—hath much of thee to say.
'Tis in its undertone, which few can hear,
Soft, sweet, and spirit-like—and O how dear!
Thus I with thee may wander evermore
The charméd paths along Potomac's shore!

Infancy.

WHEN infant loveliness departs,
  A rose-bud life's untimely doom,
Not all the rain of clouded hearts
  Can render back its bloom.

We know our tears avail not now,
  And yet we only weep the more,
And bend to kiss the little brow
  Whose answering smile is o'er.

But let them fall, these holy tears;
  In every heart a fountain lies,
That conquers first, then softens, cheers,
  And fits us for the skies!

The SON OF GOD through sorrow passed:
  And grief is love—'tis not a frown:
The crowned in Heaven find tears at last
  The jewels of the crown!

The Promise of the Age.

'TIS coming! Wheresoe'er ye be,
  Tyrants, tremble!
Like waves upon a stormy sea,
  MEN assemble!
O, ye thought them little worth!
O, ye trod them down to earth!
Ages, ages passed, and still
Bent they to your iron will,
Silent, save for helpless groans,
Curses deep, in muffled tones,
Curses—prayers! To GOD they prayed,
Wildly—even of Heaven afraid,
  Lest Heaven itself had scarcely power
   Or will to aid!
  So long they saw the darkness lower,
   The awful darkness, more than night,
   How dared they hope for light!
   But now the hour!
'Tis coming! Wheresoe'er ye be,
  Tyrants, tremble!
An earthquake! avalanche! a stormy sea!
  MEN assemble!

Ye cannot daunt—ye cannot soothe them now!
Behold! a blazing star on every brow!

Behold ! a flaming sword in every hand
    Darts judgment through the land !
  Run to your golden palaces ! Despair
    Shrieks in the perfumed air !
      Ascend the glittering throne !
Ay, play the King ! make all your terrors known !—
    That freezing voice is there !

Go forth again—clasp well your armor on,
    Bid the mad trumpet sound,
Summon your long-tried Chiefs ! What ! traitors ! gone !
    No friend—not one—is found ?
Proud Monarch ! Majesty, indeed, is thine !—
    Thy changeless diamonds shine !
No more ! no more ! Remember Nero's fate !
Ever the tyrant's ! Cringing thing of hate,
So low, so mean, even the veriest slave
Feels nobler far than thou, more good, and wise, and brave !
      Yet shrink not for thy life !
      Freedom hath better strife !
      Freedom will pass thee by ;
And if the burning glance of Freedom's eye
    Kill not at once—then live !
Were fiends to torture thee, no worse their rage could give !

  The world hath had a dream !
  Poets of every time have sung its glory,
Sages have made it still their dearest theme,
  And calm Religion smiled to hear the story !
    The world hath had a dream !
      The world awakes !
Darkness and terror now no more supreme,
    The promised morning breaks !

Beautiful dream of Liberty !
All thou hast told shall be !
America ! on thee, the first,
Hath the lovely vision burst,
And shines so fair its roseate light
That far away, through ancient night,
Look out the nations—gazing long—
  Gazing, wondering long,
While pleasures never known before,
  A strange and conquering throng,
Rise fast : " What sweetest boon to be
Like thee, our Sister ! O like thee !"

'Tis coming !   Dream of bard and sage !
    Dream the good are proud to cherish !
Heaven will grant the present age
    Joy that shall not perish !

Autumn.

IN the cloudy and windy weather,
  The time of the falling leaf,
By the stream in the mournful forest,
  I talk with my own heart's grief.

And the sound of the rock-vexed waters,
  The wind in the gloomy sky,
And the leaves in their circling dance of death—
  They all to my heart reply !

IVYWALL.

Man, in his day of sorrow,
  Seeks not the crowd of men;
Lonely and desolate places
  Alone console him then.

For brother mocketh brother,
  But Nature, with sympathy mild,
Shares the grief of the spirit,
  Like a mother soothing her child.

Her loving arms are open;
  She draws to her generous breast
All who are weary and drooping,
  And: "I will give ye rest!"

Rest!   It is all I live for,
  No other ambition now!
The crown of the world is a crown of thorns—
  Let the olive bind my brow!

"April Fool."

Who smileth not when April comes,
  And all the boys are out,
With spring-time faces, fresh and fair,
  With laugh, and leap, and shout?

Remembering Aprils long ago,
  Who smileth not again,
Feeling his heart grow young and glad
  In the midst of the joyous train?

And even the old, old man can now
  Scarce keep his trembling voice;
For thronging thoughts of youthful days
  Evermore cry, " Rejoice!"

He would shout the merry " April fool!"
  He would laugh " Ha! ha!" and run;
Of all the careless, romping crowd,
  The loudest, wildest one!

But think thee, sir! Thy locks are white,
  Thine eyes are sunken now;
So pale, and thin, and very old—
  What with these wouldst thou?

Ah, yes! he thinks—the grave old man—
  And tears are in his eyes:
" I'd rather again be an 'April fool,'
  Than the world should call me wise!"

Soldiers of 1812.

March on!   Ye are not old to-day!
  The lofty music's cheering sound
  The echo of the past hath found!
    Ye are not old to-day!

Yon banner in your line is old,
  'Tis torn and faded—pierced by balls;
  It waves—and all your youth recalls—
    And so ye are not old!

But yesterday, your step was slow,
  But yesterday, each form was bowed;
  To-day—of well-won victories proud,
    Ready again for war!

Linger among us, meek-eyed Peace!
  These who have loved thee, these who gave
  Home, friends, lost all, thy smile to save—
    Honor and bless them long!

Youth of the only Freedom Land!
  Behold!   And if the call should be
"To arms!"   March on!   To Liberty
    Your sires have shown the way!

5

Remembered Love.

Now thou dost to memory seem
Part a truth and part a dream,
For I am old, and long ago,
     Long ago,
  Were thine eyes so bright to see,
  Were thy words so soft to me !
    Now I know,
If those eyes, that won my heart,
If thy words, a bliss impart,
  Mine no more the bliss may be !

I am old, but yet, not yet,
Can my soul thy youth forget,
Can thy gentle beauty fade,
    Pine and fade—
  For the magic power of love
  Made thee like the blest above !
    Thus arrayed
In immortality of grace,
I ever see thy angel face,
  And still art thou my sorrow's dove !

Higher let the waters rise,
Let the rain fall from the skies,
Care I not; for thou, at last,
    Yes, at last,

Faithful dove! with radiant wing,
Shalt the branch of olive bring!
Then the past,
All its loneliness and fear,
All its night shall disappear!
Such will be thy welcoming!

Truth.

FROM THE FRENCH OF LEFRANC DE POMPIGNAN.

THE Nile has heard
Upon its shores the desert's dusky dwellers
By savage cries insult
The rising Star of the Universe.
Impotent cries! mad fury!
For, while these barbarous monsters
Utter their insolent clamors,
The God, pursuing his high career,
Pours torrents of still-increasing light
On his obscure blasphemers!

Thy Day is o'er.

Fare-thee-well!   We must not weep:
God Himself hath blest thy sleep,
Making it as sweet to see
As an infant's rest may be!
    God is love!

Now, good-night!   Thy day is o'er,
Smilest 'mid thy friends no more:
Smilest—ah, that winning grace!
Nevermore its joy to trace—
    Never more!

When thy star of life went out,
Many hearts were sad with doubt—
Lowly hearts, that seldom find
Lofty hearts so true and kind—
    True and kind!

Beautiful wast thou with love,
Living by the law above;
So that all who knew thee found
Earth was fairer!   Now, around,
    Blessings breathe!

Friendship.

In boyhood's artless days our friends are many.
We share each other's thoughts as freely then
As common games, and, ever, joyous dreams
Picture the future, brighter still and brighter;
Ourselves alone, of all the world, unchanged,
Or grown more dear in friendship!
      Years pass on—
And boyhood's laughing face wears sober manhood.
What tale hath Time to tell?
      We have forgotten
The comrades loved before. Each for himself
Perchance hath sought, what all around are seeking,
Wealth, fame; and this pursuit absorbs him quite.

Yet other years pass on. Sad, tottering Age—
Yea, sad, though wealth and fame are his at last—
Remembers him, still vaguely, once he had
Fond, bright-eyed friends, who made him happy—happy!
Would he were so again! Where are they now?

He learns the history of some on tombstones;
Of others by report; some dead—all gone,
To meet no more on earth. And pale and tearful,
But with a smile anon athwart his features,
He thinks of that near home, where Friendship lives,
And all the loved and lost shall be restored!
  5*

Light Coming.

I have never known perfection
   Among the sons of Earth;
Yet in every bosom lingers
   Some sign of heavenly birth.

No heart is wholly sinful,
   No thoughts are only night;
The gloom may change to glory,
   From the faintest ray of light!

The darkness of long ages,
   As time is growing old—
Do we not behold it kindle?
   Shall its progress be controlled?

Still onward—ever onward,
   Shall the joyous splendor rise,
Till the towers upon the mountains
   First reflect the golden skies.

As man, sublimely standing
   Upon the Mount of Thought,
Where the early beams of beauty
   And of blessed love are caught:

While the vale is dark beneath him,
  Yet to smile with pleasure soon—
When the still-advancing sunlight
  Shall climb toward the noon.

Yes, Earth shall be delivered
  From her multitude of foes;
And even her wildest desert
  Shall blossom as the rose!

Live on, with soul undaunted,
  Strive constantly for truth!
Restore the olden ages
  Their Paradise of Youth!

Live on, with cheerful spirit—
  Improve the passing day!
Ye are the favored sons of Time,
  And GOD commands: Obey!

Willie.

No, he would not wait to listen
  To the early birds of Spring;
Would not wait to see the fruit-trees'
  Rose and silver blossoming;
Would not wait till warmer showers,
Love-tears, should revive the flowers!

Voices, too, of home, so fondly
    Answered, but awhile ago,
Now received a sighing answer,
    Or a smile that whispered "No!"
Earth had much to bid him stay,
Still he waved the earth away!

Yes, the angels up in Heaven
    Oft had sought the gentle boy,
"Let him come to us!" entreating,
    "Let him enter in THY joy!"
And at last were satisfied :
And the world said : "Willie died!"

But our noble-hearted Willie
    Would not so forsake our love :
No, the angels lured him from us,
    For a little while, above :—
And it is not strange they should :
Willie was for us too good !

Now at last the truth is clearer;
    He will come to us no more !
But where he is, Spring is ever,
    And upon the blooming shore
Willie's welcome yet may be :
"Now, indeed, 'tis Heaven to me!"

William and Amelia.

EPITHALAMIUM.

SISTER before, and doubly Sister now,
Bride of my Brother!   By a soul-breathed vow
Thy life flows musical with his, as flow
Two sylvan brooks together.   Years ago,
Their course was near each other; day by day
Laughing along their wild, impetuous way,
Glad in the song of birds, the bloom of flowers,
Glad in the sunlight, glad in starry hours.
Thus passed they on.   I saw, with secret pride,
Near and more near their young affections glide—
But soon a parting: thus the stronger brook
Wanders away, and in a shadowy nook
The sister stream seeks solitude, and seems
Enamoured now of gentle thoughts and dreams.
At last the restless rover finding nought
To love like early love—returns; hath sought—
Hath found: " these twain are one !"

                The GOD of love
Smile ever on your pathway!   Skies above,
Be cloudless!   Still along your happy course,
Sing birds! bloom flowers! and crystal as its source
Be the re-union with that halcyon sea
Whose borders are the arms of DEITY!

The Old-time Carrier.

WHO that remembers twenty years ago
In Washington—ah, what a "city" then!
Its "distances" indeed "magnificent!"—
But readily recalls the paper-carrier?
At early morn, while yet the pavement trees
Dropped dew—or icicles—he sallied forth,
Eager to ride his "route"—to ride? ay, ride!
For then he moved in state, as doth become
His intellectual office—not, as now,
Plodding a-foot!   The messenger of truth,
Wisdom political, all grave affairs,
And sometimes gay ones, laughter-moving wit,
Sweet poesie, strange anecdote, and news
Caught in the many corners of the world—
Deserves to be exalted—well deserves!

Here at my cottage home, the "Telegraph"
This moment falls upon the garden path,
Close by the tree, beneath whose murmuring shade,
Awhile ago, I sat me down, expectant.
And 'twas the carrier of the Telegraph
Gave back to me my youth—*that* carrier
Who rode sublime on horseback—*this* who walks.
And I discovered, or I fancied so,
A likeness in the boy to him, the man—
Perhaps his father—who *my* father brought
A "Telegraph"—on horse high-mounted, brought.

Never will I forget him.   Tall he was,
And, on his Rosinante's bony back,
Nearly to earth his stirruped feet did reach.
There would he sit astride, and blow his horn
With conscious dignity, to give the house
Glad tidings of his presence!   Wondrous man!
How all the little boys would throng to see him,
And stand, and stare, admiring still the more,
Till, gathering up the reins, the majesty
Passed on, with head erect!
      Thus day by day
He rode, and made a pleasure of his task,
And when the night of Saturday arrived,
He met his comrades where the curtains red
Promised good entertainment: Royally
Raising his glass, and drinking to " the Press!"
" Kings may be blest, but Tam was glorious!"   Still
More glorious New Year's Day, when patrons all
Showered bright silver!
      And the boy 's on foot!
The son of such a sire!   Alas! alas!

But why recall the past? 'tis now a dream;
Let it sink back to darkness.   Wherefore now
Pity the boy because he may not ride?
Have I not seen, in these degenerate days,
Editors walking?

In the Night.

LATE in the night; and dimly
  Swift figures come and go,
Where, under the broad trees sombre,
  The lamps their lustre throw.

Over the sounding pavement,
  Returning home, each one,
The long, long labor ended,
  Or the wild, loud revel done.

And now and then, as passing,
  Two kindly voices greet;
A moment, and the footfalls
  Grow fainter on the street.

And some there be, who wander,
  And scarce could answer where,
Gazing up to the windows—
  For them no light is there!

But the summer stars are shining
  Sweet through the rifted cloud,
Cheering the lonely passers,
  Alike the poor and proud.

Life is a checkered pathway,
  Which joys awhile illume,
Though presently comes the shadow
  Of strange, gigantic gloom.

And man, with labor wearied,
  Thinks of his pleasant rest;
And he who is wild at the revel,
  Will scorn its highest zest.

And still dim forms are passing,
  And friendly voices greet,
Then life grows faint, departing,
  Like footfalls on the street.

And some who wander homeless,
  And steal away from the light—
To them each door is mocking,
  And a curse in each " Good-night !"—

But that the stars of promise
  Shine through the rifted cloud;
And in OUR FATHER'S mansion
  Shall none be poor or proud !

Time to go Home.

TIME to go home!   The afternoon,
The calm and golden afternoon,
O, it went so very soon!

Dancing had they been, and singing;
Thus were some, and others bringing
Flowers to deck the dancers gay,
Fairest flowers of sunny May,
That grew amid the silken grass,
Where the beautiful waters pass,
Grew upon the hill-side steep,
Grew where placid shadows sleep,
Round the border of the deep,
And dark, and still old wood.
Some—and O, the chase was good!—
A wild, and laughing, shouting chase,
Clambering now a rocky place,
Leaping now the brook, and now
Panting to the high hill's brow—
Chasing ever, ever, ever,
A butterfly, with vain endeavor,
Vain and vain—until, at last,
Their young and joyous strength is past,
And down they sink to rest—to rest
Also sinks the unpossessed,
The glorious, and the coveted—
Just a little overhead!

These are children : some there be
Old, with like simplicity,
Seeking butterflies of wealth,
Or with strides, or steps of stealth,
Chasing butterflies of fame,
Or butterflies of many a name,
Seldom caught, and little worth,
Only of a lowly birth,
Perishing upon the earth !

Time to go home !   The afternoon,
The breezy summer afternoon,
How was it that it went so soon !
Yonder comes the round, red moon !

Children, there may yet be years,
Oftener bringing clouds and tears,
Then, perchance, with upward eyes,
Then, perchance, with longing sighs,
Shall ye wait—nor wish to roam—
For the welcome summons home !

Vain the world is : yet there be
Things therein the angels see
Rejoicing : even here is Love,
A wandering smile from GOD above ;
Even on the lowly ground
Honor, Virtue, Truth are found,
Ever to their native skies
Looking up with dauntless eyes,
As calm they move their destined round.
Behold, and learn of these to rise !

Cheerfully go on through life,
Let the sun shine, let the strife
Of clouds prevail—it matters not—
For night, the night of death, shall blot
All sorrow's record : then the morn !
A free and happy soul is born,
Beyond the fearful shades of Earth—
A brighter world—a second wondrous birth !

The River.

FAR away I see thy waters,
    River of my boyhood days !
Resting now in twilight slumber,
    Canopied with purple haze.

Dark, beyond, the hills of forest
    Guard thy beautiful repose ;
Softly shines the star of evening ;
    Forth the minstrel zephyr goes.

Sadly sweet the days returning,
    Which my happy boyhood proved,
When beside thy twilight waters
    I, a minstrel lover, moved.

Thou wast half my inspiration,
　　All the rest some rosy child,
Who had lighted up my spirit
　　With her large eyes, blue and mild!

Darker grows the city round me;
　　River, thou art fading fast,
Yet I see the sky reflected,
　　See the starlight o'er thee cast.

Darker grows the world around me,
　　Soon must fade whate'er I love;
Then may Heaven be in my bosom!
　　Then the Star of Hope above!

Julia.

LADY, unto thee belong
Melodies of sacred song,
Such as only seldom rise
Underneath the daylight skies,
But in mystic dreams of night
Fill the soul with proud delight!

Oftentimes I dreamed of these
Heaven-ascending harmonies,
　6*

Till, meseemed, the Golden Gate,
Where the angel guardians wait,
Backward swung—and Heaven was there,
O, surpassing sweet and fair!
Then, awaking, still I found
Common scenes of Earth around,
Ever, till to-day—and now
Is it still the dream—or thou?

Thou, a maiden fond and young—
'Twas a mortal maiden sung!
Youth and beauty ne'er may be
So sublime a sight to see,
As when her conquering voice ascends,
While her heart with the music blends,
Voice, and heart, and beaming eyes,
Each expressing harmonies,
Which the angels love to hear,
Which to GOD HIMSELF are dear!

Genevieve.

WHITHER shall fancy wander
To find an image for thee,
Over the earth, or the heavens,
Or down in the caverned sea?

The queenly rose, or the lily,
  That shares her summer reign,
A bird, a pearl, or a diamond,
  Their charms bestow in vain.

Yet fair art thou, and noble,
  And worthy a royal name;
But more than beauty and grandeur
  Is only thy proper claim:

The true, fond soul of Woman!
  A flower from the Land of Love,
A bird that bringeth to mortals
  Music from bowers above:

A gem whose infinite value
  The world can but dimly know,
Till GOD, when HE gathers HIS jewels,
  Its Heaven-born glory show!

Rosa.

THOU hast the angel gift of beauty,
  Tint of rose adorns thy cheek,
Vermil is thy lip, and sweetly
  Do thy dark eyes speak.

Those who see thee lightly passing,
  Think of music, spring, and love,

Think of dreams that strangely wander
  Earth-ward from above.

Think—until the sorrow-shrouded,
  Sighing spirit learns to smile,
Feeling all its happy youth-days
  Thronging back the while—

Thronging back, with kind emotions,
  Kind and vast, embracing all,
Pure as sunbeams, sweet as showers
  In their summer fall !

Thus, where'er thou movest, pleasure,
  Gentleness, and virtue rise,
Proving God created beauty
  Both for heart and eyes.

Then remember, lovely maiden,
  Messenger of Heaven art thou :
Bear thee well, that still thy pathway
  Be as fair as now.

One by one, through circling seasons,
  One by one, thy charms shall go :
Yet thy home-advancing spirit
  Prouder grace may know.

This be now thy wish, thy effort ;
  Blooming Earth owns nought so bright
As the heart-rose, fondly opening
  To the " perfect light !"

The Violet.

'And now good-night, dear father,
    Good-night, and pleasant rest!'
She loved him, and her sweet young lips
    Her love with a kiss exprest:
'Good-night again, dear father!
    How very dear art thou!
A mother's and a sister's love—
    In thee I seek them now;
For both have left me, father,
    And sleep in the grave-yard green,
Where, under the drooping willow,
    The violet smiles serene—
The violet, beautiful flower!
    Should make my poor heart wise;
Though lowly, 'tis loving, and ever
    Weareth the tint of the skies!
And I, too, will look to Heaven,
    And Heaven shall be in my heart;
So again good-night, dear father—
    'Tis time, indeed, we part!
See, the moon is sinking yonder,
    Behind the dark, wild shore,
And unless I say good-night at once,
    The night will be no more!
Good-night!'

                    'Good-night, my daughter!
          God bless thee, child!   Good night!'

          The hours stole on in silence,
            And slowly came the light.

          The light that bringeth gladness—
            Yet still the maiden slept;
          A tear was on her rosy cheek,
            For in her dream she wept,
          But not a tear of sorrow—
            Her lips retained their smile,
          Like April, when the rain descends
            In sunshine all the while.
          Perchance she had been dreaming
            Of those she loved—the dead—
          When joy came up with her father's look,
            And sighing fancies fled.

          The light that bringeth gladness—
            It dawned: the father slept:
          The parting smile of blessing
            His aged face still kept.
          And presently, to see it,
            The gentle maiden woke,
          And bent above his slumber,
            And morn's glad greeting spoke.
          O, sweet and tender accents!
            'Twas music, all she said:
          But still no loving answer—
            She bent above the dead!

The violet, beautiful flower!
  The violet smiles serene,
Under the drooping willow,
  Within the grave-yard green.
'Tis lowly, 'tis loving, and ever
  Weareth the tint of the skies,
Teaching a lonely maiden,
  And making her sad heart wise.
' And I, too, will look to Heaven,
  And Heaven shall be in my heart;
And the morning will come, dear father,
  When we no more shall part!'

The Maid of the Mountain.

I left the city, and the mountain land
  Was like another world. I climbed the height,
And from a vine-clad ruin saw expand
  The vale, in beauty of the sunset light.
  Descending then I wandered where a bright
Impetuous brook ran gracefully along,
And lured me still with laughter-mingled song.

I rested underneath the grand old trees,
  I read—I wrote the strange-inspired rhyme;
Music was round me, with the birds—the breeze
  With sweets of Paradise. And thus the time
  Went happily. Far off, the blue sublime

Of mountain-peaks was all the while so fair,
Meseemed 'twas Heaven, and angels hovered there!

Yet came a pleasure dearer than the rest:
  I found a fair young girl, whose loving heart
Was tuned to poesie. My heart confessed
  Its joy complete. And still I must depart.
  I go, but pause a moment ere I start,
To bless thee, and to wish thee golden days,
Heaven-lit, till Heaven itself reward thy upward gaze!

Loueva.

  The flowers and trees, at Ivywall,
  The birds and breeze, at Ivywall,
    Are pleasant things,
    But (less the wings)
  An angel comes to Ivywall!

  On velvet ground, at Ivywall,
  With ivy bound, at Ivywall,
    When skies are bright,
    The hours of light
  The dial tells, at Ivywall.

  A seat is made, at Ivywall,
  Within the shade, at Ivywall;
    Loueva there
    Enchants the air,
  And time's forgot, at Ivywall!

The winding walks, at Ivywall,
·The changeful talks, at Ivywall!
        The charms appear
        Of Eden here—
An angel comes to Ivywall!

Absence.

DEATH and absence so resemble—
    Now, my love, thou art away,
When I think of thee, I tremble,
    Lest thou 'rt gone for aye!

Here, among my books, I wait thee,
    Books and pictures, dear to me;
Come, my love, and gladness freight thee,
    Home-bound, o'er the sea.

Could'st thou know how sad my heart is,
    In the midnight, here, alone—
Could'st thou know how poor a part is
    Life without my Own!—

Could'st thou see me read thy letters,
    Lingering on each glowing line,
Till the cruel Now makes fetters
    Even of flowers divine!—

        7

Could'st thou see my friends around me—
　　How I strive to talk and smile,
Feeling still new tortures wound me,
　　More, and more, the while—

How, when friends, at last, departing,
　　Awfully the silence lowers,
And, like one distraught, up-starting,
　　How I moan the hours !

How I chide my wayward madness,
　　Saying : " Peace, O peace, my soul !
Take the harp !　Therein is gladness !
　　Taste the wreathéd bowl !"

But no more my soul obeys me,
　　But no more the harp is sweet,
But the wreathéd bowl betrays me,
　　With a strange deceit !

Yonder landscape, golden bordered,
　　Is it not as charming still ?
No !　Its colors, all disordered—
　　Who could paint so ill !

Here 's a page with beauty beaming,
　　Like a crystal, summer tide,
While below its fair waves, gleaming,
　　Diamond truths reside.

No !　It is a fickle beauty,
　　Not for me such beauty cold ;

And its "diamond truths" of duty—
　　Give them to the old!

Hark! the wind-harp!　Rising, falling!
　　Hath the world such dulcet strain!
Is it not some spirit calling
　　Wanderers home again!

Now no more it brings me pleasure,
　　Though my fond delight before :—
Wilt thou whisper him of treasure
　　Who hath lost his glittering store!

．

Birth-Day.

How long it takes to die!
　　My laboring breath
　　Draws nearer death.
　　　　A cry,
　　　　A sigh,
Thus begins, and thus goes on,
　　Life—the strange!
　　Then a change—
　　A groan, and life is gone!

Toys of childhood please me not,
Toys of later years forgot,

What may coming years bestow?—
  If such coming years be mine?
Toys! which I may live to throw
    Away,
    Some wiser day—
And then for new ones pine!

Life is not the end of life;
  If it were, how sad to live!
Doubt, and fear, and wrong, and strife—
  What boon were this to give!

Cease, my soul, and know thy fetter
  Now not long shall bind thee here:—
Time hath worn it. Soon a better,
    Happier sphere,
Shall be thine, set free forever,
Rising still, aweary never,
    Till to thee,
  All the grandeur, all the grace
  Of the FATHER's smiling face
In highest Heaven revealed shall be!

Take, then, take the gifts of life,
  Well remembering HIM who gave.
Doubt, and fear, and wrong, and strife—
  Are they ills? or meant to save?

He who wanders in the night,
  Having yet a faithful GUIDE,
Shall he say: "It is not right!"
  Shall he turn aside?

Agnes, " The Fairy Star."

A dream of beauty, gentleness, and love,
  Comes to all hearts, for Heaven such light bestows,
That images the charm of worlds above,
  And smiles away the earth-born cloud of woes.
  By day, by night, the radiant vision goes,
Whispering from heart to heart; and now the tone,
  Or now the smile, is all the dreamer knows,
Save that the dream of Heaven to Heaven hath flown.
Rest thee, fair spirit! leave us not alone!
  Longing, we look, and, listening, learn of thee—
Agnes, of thee! for, answering our hearts' moan,
  Heaven said : " Let beauty live!   Let Agnes be!"
Love-dream's reality! yet dream-like still !
Thy diadem a smile, thy realm the heart and will!

7*

Love.

THE love of which the poets sing
Is but a flower, a fragile thing,
Nursed by many a smile and tear,
Yet doomed to die before the year!

'Tis beautiful to see—and so
Is yonder many-colored bow,
That springs among the showery shades,
And in its sudden grandeur—fades!

The love most worthy poets' song
Is also fair, and liveth long,
It blossoms, ripens day by day,
And winter takes not all away.

Sweet is the fruit of blesséd love!
Like manna sent by GOD above,
When hope no otherwhere is found,
What instant joy it spreads around!

The light of love is like the sun,
Or like the moon, when day is done,
Or like the stars—for still a light
For love shines, e'en in darkest night!

And love shall never want on earth,
And love shall have a brighter birth,
The moment it may vanish here—
Triumphant in a deathless sphere!

Joe Tremble.

SULTRY the day was, though a day in Spring-time,
One of those days that suddenly come on us,
Making us feel luxuriously lazy,
            Nothing inclined to:

Nothing at all, unless, with chair tilted,
Feet on the window-sill, head cushioned softly,
Through smoke of cigar good, forth to gaze, sleepy,
            Wondering at passers:

Wondering that any for pleasure should walk now,
Pitying any whom business out-urges,
Yet smoothing the while the beard of the spirit,
            That *we* can be idle!

Such was the season, and such the position,
Up in his garret, Joe Tremble, Esquire, had

Taken, in comfort to pass the dull hour, and
        Smoke after dinner!

Joe was a Clerk—had for six months, and over,
Served our great Country, and paid his own debts off—
Monthly instalments—till now they were paid all,
        Minus ten dollars.

So, he was thinking of next happy "pay day,"
And how, when his creditors ceased to be creditors,
Careful of money, he'd save, and get married—
        Yes—and get married!

Further I tell not: but there he sat, smoking,
Smoke all around him, still rising, and rising,
Out from the window up-curling, and mounting
        Slow to the chimney.

Down on the pavement some boys were at marbles,
Near, at the pump, stood a girl with a bucket:
The marbles stopped rolling—the bucket ran over—
        A dog began barking.

Alarm rose of "fire!"—grew louder and louder—
Engine-bell joined it, and swift came the engine—
Pump-handle rattled—a strong stream dashed upward—
        Dousing Joe Tremble!

Knew he nought of it until that wild moment!
Tumbled he over, and dripping retreated,
Bounding down stairs in alarming commotion,
        Spraining his ankle!

Crowded the hall was, with furniture various,
Crowded the pavement with ditto:—he cleared it—
Breaking a mirror—appalling the movers—
   Flying and screaming!

Thus was cold water dashed over his musing;
Thus—for Joe Tremble, Esquire, was timid—
Lost he his loved-one, who laughed at him, so that
   He would no more see her!

Reader! whoever thou art, be attentive!
Ponder the evils that issue from smoking!
Sad to lose lady-love—shocking is water-cure!
   Think of Joe Tremble!

Marriage.

To-day, this hour, in fair Virginia's land,
 My friends have spoken love's eternal vow;
Heart hath been pledged to heart, and hand to hand:
 These two are one, let none divide them now!

Sweet is the rising of the light of love,
 Gladness goes with it on its brightening way,
Hymns of the happy hail it from above,
 And God's own smile crowns it with perfect day.

Evil, that hid among the Eden bowers,
　　With hot breath blasted all the garden's charm,
The tall trees drooped, and death struck pale the flowers,
　　But love grew fonder in the strange alarm.

Love went from Eden, yet where'er love went
　　Was Eden still, and still where love shall go,
Beauty and joy shall cheer its banishment,
　　And Evil weep his ineffectual woe.

The Child.

CHILD of my childhood's friend,
　　I 've seen thee first to-night :
Thy tiny lips were wreathed with a smile,
　　And thine eyes were softly bright.

Joyous wast thou to hear
　　Thy father's fondling song ;
Joyous to see thy mother's face,
　　With its love-look sweet and long !

Over thee still may shine
　　Affection's heavenly ray !
May it light thy path o'er the dangerous Earth,
　　And guide to "the better way !"

Rosa Maye of Ivywall.

Rosa Maye of Ivywall!
Ah, the dreams her looks recall!
But none may be so sweet as she,
    My Rosa Maye of Ivywall!
The Graces, with their circling arms,
  As something all divine enclose her,
And so admire her heavenly charms,
  They even forget to envy Rosa!
    Rosa Maye of Ivywall!

Rosa Maye of Ivywall!
Beauty's smiles are joy to all,
But bliss above the looks of love
    Hath Rosa Maye of Ivywall!
What though the world may call her queen,
  My heart a prouder title owes her,
And one true heart is more, I ween,
  Than thousand thrones to gentle Rosa!
    Rosa Maye of Ivywall!

Summer Holiday.

FAR from the city's stifling heat,
  I found a green, sequestered shade.
The cedar-scented winds were sweet;
The waters, murmuring at my feet, .
      Allured me down the glade.

In grandeur stood the brave oak trees,
  In beauty grew the flowering vine;
Here, would the waving harvest please,
There, butterflies, and birds, and bees :
      A glad new world was mine!

I gave my soul to pleasure then,
  I gazed upon the earth, the sky.
The weary, weary " haunts of men,"
My ceaseless task of book or pen,
      Went like a vision by.

That vision went, another came,
  The fairest that may ever be!
A maiden, with a gentle name,
Fond " Mary," dearest yet to fame,
      In far-voiced poesie!

Ah then, what charms the landscape caught!
 What softer colors glowed above!
For earth and sky at once were fraught
With graces of commingled thought,
     And eloquence of love!

Hereafter, when the boon is mine
 To look on Nature's summer pride,
A consecrated light shall shine
To cheer my soul—for, Mary, thine
     Will then before me glide!

God is Ours.

LIFE is passing, passing fleetly,
 Yet to music let it go;
Heaven is pleased to see it sweetly,
     Gaily flow:
Joy on earth is praise above;
And our FATHER's name is Love!

Beautiful the world around us:
 If terrific shades of ill
Sometimes in their chain have bound us:
     "Peace! be still!"
Shades they are, and only shades:
Lo, the chain dissolves and fades!
  8

What are these our arms entwining?
  Not the iron links—but flowers!
Shall we question GOD's designing?
      GOD is ours!
We are HIS: and FATHER, child,
Loving much, are reconciled!

In HIS glory, all-excelling,
  Looks HE down, well pleased to see
Joy illume our lowly dwelling!
      Let it be!
They are wrong who speak of woe:
Let our life to music flow!

Where is Scotland?

SPOKEN AT THE ANNUAL CELEBRATION OF ST. ANDREW'S SOCIETY, WASHINGTON, 1859.

WHERE is Scotland?   In the North,
  In the wintry regions,
Where the thunder-voicéd storm
  Calls his cloudy legions!

Where is Scotland?   In the South,
  In the land of flowers,
Where immortal summer smiles
  In her orange bowers!

Where is Scotland?   In the East,
  By the sun's appearing,
Beautiful beneath the palm,
  Eden's sorrow cheering!

Where is Scotland?   In the West,
  By the sun's declining,
Freedom's GOD-built dome above,
  And her pure stars shining!

Scotland! Scotland! every where!
  Where is told the story
How the Bruce of Bannockburn
  Fought for deathless glory!

Scotland! Scotland! every where!
  Where the heart of maiden
Throbs to hear the song of Burns,
  Love and rapture laden!

Scotland! like thy circling waves,
  Wide and wide extending,
Now thou dost embrace the world,
  Power and beauty blending!

Scotland! hail! across the sea!
  Scorner of foul weather!
Scotland! hail! where two or three
  Of thine are met together!

Age.

My heart is so much younger than my face,
   That I am startled when myself I see,
And cannot on the mirror's surface trace
   Save a poor counterfeit resembling me.
The snows of time that rest upon my head,
   Fall from a beautiful and smiling sky,
While earth in summer pomp is garnishéd,
   And dreams of glory glide serenely by.
Thus in the world the world esteems me old,
   But thus, despite the world, I am not so;
My summer heart laughs at the winter's cold,
   My rose of life looks blooming through the snow.
The lamp hath stains of age, and may be broken;
The light—from God—is an eternal token!

Indian Burial.

A picture by J. M. STANLEY, in the Smithsonian Institution. It has attracted much attention, not only for the singular custom of placing the dead among the boughs of a tree, but for the pathos and poetry of the whole composition. In such subjects STANLEY is without a rival.

YES, ye are there!   Beneath the tree
  Whose fading leaves, in evening's breath,
  Sing, faintly sing, the song of death,
    And tell how brave was he!

Yes, ye are there!   Ye mourn the dead,
  The warrior form above ye placed,
  His last sad home by flowers embraced,
    The light boughs round it spread.

Last of your race!—The white-haired sire—
  How desolate is age in grief!
  Where now thy pride, O, mighty Chief!
    Where now· thy battle fire!

Weary to thee the world is now,
  Love, war, no more may move thy breast;
  And yet one heart is more distressed—
    The mother more than thou!

He was *her* child.   His infant smile,
  His earliest word—they were for her
    8*

Love's light, and joy's interpreter,
    And earth was Heaven the while.

In after years, his manly form
    Was pride to thee—to her 'twas love;
    Her soul was near him like the dove—
        Thine, like the rushing storm!

Yet, mother of the brave departed,
    Thou bendest over one who bore
    More love for him—yes, mother, more!
        And is more broken-hearted!

His wife!   Her face is hidden low,
    Her prostrate attitude is grief,
    Down to the earth!   For thy relief
        Hope may be!   Hers—ah, no!

He who is dead, thou gavest him life,
    Therefore for him thy love was great;
    He who is dead—her soul's lost mate—
        Mother, she was his wife!

On the soft bosom of yon cloud,
    Glowing in sunset's parting ray,
    Behold!   'Tis gliding now away!
        Manito's truth avowed!—

A dove.   His spirit!   Grieve it not!
    Manito to the sorrowing heart
    Sends comfort!   Therefore, rise, depart,
        And be your tears forgot!

Our Native Land.

AMERICA! the glory
  Of the Golden Age is thine:
The nations gaze upon thee
  As a wonder and a sign.

The Roman Eagle, victor
  On a thousand crimson plains—
Thy Eagle hath outflown it,
  And thy victory remains!

It shall remain forever!
  It shall be a kindling star,
Which the Sages, still up-looking,
  Shall honor from afar!
Till its lustre in their bosoms
  Wake a thrilling sense of joy
Which the Past hath never given,
  Nor the Future can destroy!

Thy victory is freedom!
  And it was not won alone
For the mighty, but the humble
  May the blessing also own.
It is sweet as summer sunshine,
  It is liberal as air;
From Heaven it came, and fondly
  Doth it smile and whisper: "There!"

In the time of doubt and peril,
    When the soul was sad and still
In the dreaming of the coming
    Of a vague and awful ill,—
Then the beauty and the glory
    And the blessedness were thine!—
And the nations gaze upon thee
    As a wonder and a sign!

By the sacred shades of Vernon,
    Where our Father's ashes rest;
By the name to freedom dearest!
    By our Wonder of the West!
Arise! and swear, my brothers,
    That our native land shall be
Still the hope of Earth's redemption,
    Still the happy and the free!

America! the glory
    Of the Golden Age is thine:
The nations gaze upon thee
    As a wonder and a sign!

The Dream and the Awaking.

LIFE was dreaming, life was dreaming—smiling, dreaming,
    day and night!
Beautiful its visions ever, ever changing, ever bright,
Like a placid river flowing—like the sacred river going
Gladly through the Eden Land—all the graceful, all the
    grand,
Mirrored in its buoyant bosom—all the angel-haunted land!

Life was dreaming, dreaming, dreaming : star-crowned
    forms of sweetest seeming
Hovered round—their dark eyes beaming fairer still than
    starry light,
While their white arms waving gently, while their fond
    lips' music tone,
Still invited, still delighted, promised still a joy unknown,
Saying : " Love and fame await thee, love and fame that
    shall create thee
Pride and power beyond a monarch's nation-overshadowing
    throne—
These are thine, and thine alone !"

Life, 'twas thus thy early season passed in dreams—it
    wakes to reason,
Knowing, now, those dreams were treason, treason to thy
    nobler charge :

Knowing, now, the Lord bestoweth life a loan ; thy spirit
    oweth
Right return, which overfloweth—be the Glorious Will
    obeyed !—
Still and still it *overfloweth*, blessing all thy Sovereign
    made !

Action ! action ! not for dreaming !   Learn the true intent
    of Life !
Rise ! the world is mad in battle ! on ! amid the fearful
    strife !
Brothers art thou now beholding !—Banner of the Cross
    unfolding—
Even the Banner which the Roman, marching to attack
    his foeman,
Crouching low in trembling awe, in the blazing heavens
    saw—
In hoc signo vinces !   Virtue, doubt thou not, shall conquer
    all :
Rise ! with heart and hand assist her : then shall her op-
    pressors fall—
Shrouded by their deeds of darkness, ever, ever, ever fall !

Washington Crossing the Delaware.

(LEUTZE'S PAINTING.)

WONDERFUL Art, whose bright Aurora finger
  Moves o'er the darkness of the ages past,
  Till from their cold, sepulchral regions vast
Up-springs the light again!   And long-lost faces
Appear, and live in old familiar places,
And great events of many a pondered story
Return, and re-enact their world-inspiring glory!

Winter: all grey and ghastly comes the morning!
  All desolate, obscure, and scarcely day;
  The snow-cloud hovering o'er its feeble ray,
Like an oppressor o'er the rise of freedom!

The ice, in anger clashing,
  Mass against mass; but bravely still,
  Each look, each vein, breathing immortal will,
There, in the rough-rocked boat, they toil, they go
Safe through the drift confused: wary and slow,
And silently, yet hopeful.   Gazing out,
Stands WASHINGTON!   If any heart feel doubt,
Behold the Chief—behold the kindling eye—
The " soul in arms!"—and read a grand reply!

Struggling amid the ice, boat follows boat;
An army moves—but no triumphal note

Of clarion soundeth : on the chilly air
          No banners float;
One, only, rises there,
Flapping about the staff, impatiently
          Contending with the breeze,
          As if old memories,
          Haunting its every fold,
Awoke the joy wherewith it led the bold,
          Who shall be free!

And yet, though wanting all the pomp of war,
          To victory pass they on,
          Ere the perfected dawn.
The tale hath History told—but words are weak,
And may not with the pencil's eloquence speak,
Whose rainbow language, bending down with thought,
With truth and fancy, love and beauty fraught,
Ascends the heavens, reposes on the land,
Is ever graceful, and is ever grand!

Unknown.

WHEN artists represent their dreams
  Of more than mortal grace,
Though glory in the picture beams,
  Yet nought distinct we trace:
A soft, a melting, waving line—
  A mass of shadowy hair—
Large eyes, sweet eyes, that look divine—
  Dreamlike, the dream is there!

I think of thee; I know thee not;
  Perchance I ne'er may know:
But thou art woman; and thy lot,
  Or be it high or low,
Yet is it noble, grand, sublime;
  Its mission from above,
To soothe the thousand ills of time,
  And bless the world with love!

So seemest thou, fair maiden, bright
  With charms the angels own,
That, like the breeze, like flowers, like light,
  Are joys wherever known!
A soft, a melting, waving line—
  A mass of shadowy hair—
Large eyes, sweet eyes, that look divine—
  Dreamlike, the dream is there!

Supreme.

THE LORD!   Whose sovereign Word,
Amazed, old Chaos heard,
And shrank away!
While world succeeding world
Its wondrous charms unfurled,
And hailed the Day!
To HIM whose dwelling is Eternity,
To HIM, forever, let all glory be!

And thou, my startled Soul,
What fearest thou?   Control
Thy timid thought!
Is there not rapture here
To smile away thy fear:
Thy love is sought!
HE, the CREATOR, stooping from above,
Looks through the shining spheres, and asks " thy love!"

Let not the stories old,
By priest and bigot told,
Thy trust affright!
Forgive them, and forget:
GOD is thy FATHER yet!
All shall be right!
Hell is a madman's dream, nor shall be found;
Fiends are the talk of fools!   The LORD is crowned!

CREATOR! MONARCH! FRIEND!
Who shall with HIM contend!
Whatever is,
All that we know, and more
Than mortal may explore,
All—all are HIS!
Shall HIS own creatures then torment HIS own?
Shall they o'ermaster HIM, and mount HIS awful throne?

No scowling form of Wrath
Shall haunt thy future path,
For GOD is thine!
With HIM shall love remain,
To HIM shall grief and pain
Their power resign;
For they on Earth—in Heaven we yet may know—
Were friends, though in the dark we thought not so!

A Dreamy Mood.

Now from the lattice gazing on the day,
The red and golden evening of the day,
As darker blue becomes the faint-starred sky,
As purple shades steal slowly o'er the ground,
As, now and then, some weary step goes by—
No other living form, no other sound:

Now from the lattice of my lonely room
I look upon the day's half joy, half gloom,
And scenes of long ago return to me,
And sweet love-smiles I never more may see,
And voices that were music once; and truth,
The angel in the Paradise of youth!

Rivers and mountains, even the ocean wild,
The ocean, strange, and dark, and deep, and wild,
    Keep from me dearest hearts whose vows I heard,
        Whose vows I answered with an equal vow;
    Memory alone repeats each sacred word,
        But not the same: it is with sorrow now.
And fondest of them all was hers, whose voice—
Hast thou not seen the mariner rejoice
At " Land ! land, ho !"   For thus her welcome tone
Once charmed my spirit, when, the deep unknown,
Compassed with storms, the stars I trusted, lost,
My life from wave to wave was madly tossed !

She, too, is far away—I know not so—
I see her not, and yet—I know not so:—
    Her home is Heaven; but may she not look down ?
        May not her glorious wings be folded here ?
    Is 't not her light that dissipates my frown,
        This cloud of wrong repining?   Why appear
All things more cheerful to me now, more just,
Waking within my heart a holy trust,
Teaching that parting, even death, may be
Most wise, most kind, as thus at once we see
Two worlds to live for !   Hopefully in this,
Yet with a longing for the world of bliss !

Kossuth.

—— "Back-wounding Calumny
The fairest virtue strikes."
SHAKSPEARE.

TYRANT and coward slave!
Rail on! thou mayst not harm the good and brave!
 As looks the sovereign mountain down,
 As smiles the rainbow o'er the tempest's frown,
 So looks and smiles the brave!
He stands secure, GOD's pyramid of Truth!
 Scorning the rage of Time!
He smiles—an immortality of youth,
 Peace, joy, and love sublime,
 Is there!
Circling the world, illuming all the air!

When Freedom's fire descends upon the heart,
 The man no more is man!
He feels his sacred life is set apart:—
 He feels new hope, new power,
 And from that rapturous hour
He dares do all—that tyrants fear he can!

What giveth grandeur to the mountain proud?
It is the envious, vain-aspiring cloud,
That, stealing from the pestilential vale,
Slow creepeth up—then, when its efforts fail
 9*

To shroud the dauntless peak,
How, like a coward arrogant and weak,
    Doth it descend in tears,
Back to its darkened den, its sluggish, base compeers !

What giveth beauty to the rainbow's form ?
'Tis that it shineth 'mid the sullen storm !
    Smiling as terrors cease,
    And prophesying peace !

Thou art the mountain tall, the rainbow thou !
    Herald of Freedom to the sad old World !
Shame shall attend whoe'er would cloud thy brow !
    Back on himself shall all his wrath be hurled !
        Stand he among the great,
        Or sit in royal state,
    Beyond the sea—or here :—
No, my blest Native Land ! thou art too dear,
    Too honored—even in a moment's dream
        That thus I think of thee :
No son of thine so deeply damned may be !
    I'll not believe it !   If, at last, there seem
        Such on our happy shore—
Call the false phantom " brother " never more !
    Let him accurséd be, wherever found !
    Still let him live, still let him wander round
        The unfriending Earth,
Weeping with tears of fire his day of birth ;
Or, if he have companion—legends tell
        Of one to suit him well :
        Ahasuerus, wild with awful dread,
Outcast, in search of calm—eternal clouds o'erhead !

The Haunted Clerk.

Job Smith had toiled from nine o'clock to three:
There was no wearier Job in all the "States" than he!
Figures he loved not, yet 'twas his to *add*,
Till the long columns nearly drove him mad!
Up-rose he then, at last, and strode the floor,
    Once, twice, and thrice, to stretch his aching legs,
      Which done, from off the pegs,
He took his hat and coat, and passed the office door.
      So awful were his features,
      The boys—poor little creatures!—
Amid their game of leap-frog stopped,
And hoops forgot to roll, and marbles dropped,
And mouths came open wide, and large wild eyes
Grew larger, wilder, with a mute surprise,
      As thus Job spoke:
      " Once more!
Five hundred—forty—fifty—ninety-four,
And eight——What was it? Ninety? ninety? What?
      Over and over! . There! another blot!
      'Out, damnéd spot!'
      My knife! my knife!
I cannot bear this worse than tread-mill life!"

All passers by with sadness saw his face,
  Women did pity him, and hasten on,

Doctors, with eager eyes, pronounced " the case "
　" Doubtful "—" a strange neglect "—and " nearly gone ! "

" And eight—What was it?　Ninety? ninety?"　So,
With long, unconscious strides, did Job right homeward go.

Arrived, his little son ran forth to meet him,
With chubby, dimpled arms spread wide to greet him,
　　　　Exclaiming : " Pa, to-night !
　　The circus !　Aint it time to go ?"
　　　　　　　　　　" Not quite !
　What was it ?"
　　　　　" Circus, Pa !"
　　　　　　　　" The Circus—eight "—
" No, Pa, it 's seven.　You'd be an hour too late !"
　　　—" And ninety? ninety what?
Five hundred—forty—fifty—ninety—blot !"

That evening Job went not from home, but sat,
Lost in reflection, like a sober cat,
Some stormy night, before a farmer's fire,
That nods her head—the flames mount high and higher—
That nods her head so solemnly, but keeps
Talking unto herself : think not she sleeps !

To bed at last goes Job—and silent all,
So still you might have heard a needle fall :
And thus the midnight hour—when Job's dear wife
Was roused—she trembled for her very life !

　　　With cap on head,
There in the moonbeams Job sat up in bed !

Open his eyes were, but with such a look,
As if no sense of mortal things he took :
Open his mouth was, but therefrom there came
Sounds that were Hebrew to his awe-struck dame :
" Five hundred—forty—fifty—ninety-*four!*
And eight—SIX HUNDRED TWO !"   He spake no more,
But sank upon his couch, and soon began to snore !

Kiss Me.

KISS me, sweet !   I will not tell !
Ah, I love thee quite too well
To sit beside thee patiently—
Ever so thou temptest me !

Give me, then, one little kiss,
And I will give thee—what for this ?
Richest gold could never pay it,
Clearest gems would vain essay it :
I, therefore, will return thee thine,
And a thousand more of mine !

The Doom of Death.

"THE GOOD OLD TIMES—ALL TIMES WHEN OLD ARE GOOD!"

"THE Law allows it, and the Court awards it!"
So, every true and thoughtful man regards it
Justice beyond compare!
                              Is reverence dead?
Are all our filial obligations fled?
Shall we prove false to fathers wise of old,
So light their solemn meditations hold,
As question now the law?   Dear Piety!
Forbid so foul a wrong should ever be!
Touch not the law!   It is a holy thing!
Of what proud blessings is it not the spring!
How sweet in spirit, how in moral grand!
How doth it save from crime our Christian land!

Out upon those who prate of prison gloom,
Where murderous hearts should meet a life-long doom,
Silent and terrible—a conscious death,
Having no more of earth save only breath,
And thought—thought—thought—eternal, restless thought:
A cell by mortal friendship never sought;
Yet one fond visiter admitted there,
If summoned by the voice of contrite prayer!
Then if, some day, perchance—strange things may be,
And are on record!—proof should set him free,

Law may atone for wrong the law hath done,
And cloudless sink at last life's sacred sun !
Out upon those !   Be still, the foolish tongue !
Be ours the crimson law from reason sprung !

Spirit of Innovation, blind and wrong,
Yet in its madness is it wondrous strong,
Grasping, as Sampson did, the pillars, so
To crush in ruin all the throng below :
But solemn men, inspired by truth, have risen,
And forced the giant back again to prison,
Have spoken from the BOOK—though some declare,
In foolishness, no text of blood is there !—
And, armed with power that holds the world in awe,
Have firmly fixed our consecrated law !

Alas, the present age ! alas, the zeal
Once so exhaustless for the common weal !
Still, to this day, we should behold expire
The Church-defying heretic in fire !
Still, to this day, the impious witch should burn,
The water drown, the wheel of torture turn !
The blood-stained rack the quivering limbs should tear,
While groans, and shrieks, and curses fill the air !
To prove how dear to man is virtue's claim !
To prove the glory of the Christian name !
Still, to this day, we should reward all crimes
In the sweet fashion of the good old times !

The Wife of Kossuth.

THE World hath men it doth not truly know;
The World doth often give the doom of foe
　　　Even to its fondest friend:
Chains bind the arms, and cruel tortures rend
　　The very heart-strings that were nerved to save
　　Liberty, Virtue, from the yawning grave!
　　　　'Tis sad to read the story,
Throughout all time, how Wrong hath murdered Glory!

When, far away in fair Hungaria's land,
Kossuth stood foremost of a small, brave band,
　　　For Freedom, Heaven-designed
The first and still best gift to all mankind,
　　　Sweet was the oratory—yet received
　　　　Only by few the flame;
　　　　While many, as they came,
Went back, and muttered: 'We have not believed!'
Then yet once more returned—repentant? No!
　　　Freedom's Apostle was a dangerous foe!
Bear him to prison!　And he bowed his head,
　　　　His heart unbowed,
　　And, silent, through the mocking crowd,
Moved on, with pensive, melancholy tread.

An angel came unto him!　What is love
Less than a starry spirit from above?

The smile of Woman cheered his prison cell;
The voice of Woman whispered: 'Hope! 'Tis well!'

It was!   The hero's soul grew daily stronger!
    The time of darkness gave him nobler light!
Whatever dread the past had known—no longer
    Dared now oppose his might!

It was!   He left the massive walls of gloom,
    For woman's palace-heart,
    Bright home, outrivalling the sculptor's art,
All beauty—bliss—and breathing Eden bloom!

'Twas well!   He fought his Nation's claim:
    Freedom was proud to see her flag unfurled!
He fought—and though he lost his patriot aim—
    He won the World!

For a Dial.

LIFE shall fade away, but I,
Smiling still, see shadows fly!

Answers Life: My smile shall be,
When sun nor shade exist for thee!

10

Joys of the Cottage.

Yes, boast of your splendor!   Not for me
The pomp, the pain of the palace be!
Dearer by far is the lowly roof!
    Sweeter by far is my simple life!
From the home of my heart keep all aloof
    Fashion, and pride, and their train of strife!
At my garden-gate they may stand and sneer,
But they come not in—it is sacred here!

Sacred it is to peace and to love!
Sealed with the seal of God above!
Whisper a blessing the beautiful trees!
    Ever a blessing exhales from the flowers!
Blessing is breathed by the birds and the breeze!
    By the sun, and the moon, and the rainbow showers!
And the souls that inhabit my Eden of home
With a blessing look up to the world-lighted dome!

' Is it summer forever?' a voice replies.
    Yes, for the summer within us lies—
    Happy within us: and storms may blow,
    Striking the boughs of the icicled oak,
Rattling its treasure of gems on the snow,
    And shouting the louder the fiercer the stroke:
The clouds and the cold that take blessings away,
Give others, give brighter and better than they!

Let fall the large curtains, and gather around :
Now hath the storm but a musical sound !
Cheerily sparkles the joy-giving fire !
   The lamp throws its lustre on paintings and books.
Winter—where is it?   Its rigors retire,
   And summer, soft-breathing, how peaceful it looks !
Thus should a home be !   And thus being, is it
A Paradise angels of Heaven might visit !

Moneylover.

Job Moneylover went to sea,
   Tempted by a speculation.
A storm arose, and momently
   Was death in expectation :
And " O, my gold !" not " life," cried he.

Gathering up his coins in haste—
   The big waves leaping all around him—
He girdled them about his waist,
   Went over, and his treasure drowned him,
Eagerly by the sea embraced.

O, sea ! thou takest to thy breast
   One whom the land would never cherish ;
Yet, tossed and tossed, he shall not rest,
   And though he die, he shall not perish—
Thy golden-girdled grinning guest !

Through all thy caverns green and dark
Thou 'lt bear his skeleton of terror,
Bidding thy myriad monsters mark
The master-work of human error:
" Ha! ha!" shall laugh the ravenous shark!

Still, upon his native shore,
A monument to Moneylover
Says: " He visited the poor"—
Yes, severely; they 'll recover
From his visitings no more.

Says: " As husband, father, friend,
Now on earth not one is like him!"
So, thank Heaven! and there an end.
Being down, we will not strike him,
But let his quarreling heirs defend.

Oriental Traditions.

ARABIAN.

I.

In Eden grew
Trees whose fruit was gold,
Trees that silver bore,
And others precious stones.
Beneath their beautiful boughs

First whispered Sin to man.
So, from the view of Heaven,
From sunshine, moon, and stars,
　　These trees are banished,
　　And buried deep, O deep
In the fiery caves of earth.
　　Beware thou seek them not!

II.

　　THE health-restoring plants
Sprang from the bitter tears of penitence
By Adam wept upon the accurséd earth,
　　　Through him accurséd,
During his first sad century of exile.

　　The lovely, fragrant flowers,
　　The aromatic shrubs,
Sprang from the tears of gratitude
　　　By Eve and Adam shed,
During their second century of exile,
　　　Finding their prayers were heard,
　　　Their sorrowing vows accepted.

Jane M'Cree.

Listen to the story old,
  Still, where Hudson's waters glide,
Tearfully, in whispers told,
  How a maiden loved and died.
The rosebud that adorned her breast,
Her fairer, softer charms confessed;
And kind as beautiful was she,
The loved and loving Jane M'Cree!
    So fair and fond, so young and gay,
      The absent soldier's promised bride!
    Alas! the dark and woful day!
      Alas! the death she died!

Far amid the forest lone,
  With her silent Indian guides,
Trustfully, the girl hath gone :—
  O, her heart is like a bride's!
The path is wild, but still above
Brightly beams the sky with love!
What happy meeting soon shall be!
Thy lover listens, Jane M'Cree!

On, and on, through all the day,
  Down the vale, and o'er the height!
On, and on, a weary way,
  Resting by the fire at night—

On, and on :—but words of wrath,
Serpent-like, surprise the path !
Now, the quivering dagger see !—
Ah ! the lovely Jane M'Cree !

The soldier heard the tale of woe—
   Heard as if he did not hear :
Agony may never know
   E'en the solace of a tear !
He sought the sad and fatal ground ;
He gazed upon the maiden's mound ;
He called : " I come, my love, to thee !
The world is dark for Jane M'Cree !"
      So fair and fond, so young and gay,
        The soldier and his promised bride !
      Alas ! the woful, woful day !
        They slumber side by side !

Earth's Last Angel.

WOMAN is earth's last angel !   Eden still
   With glory shines about her :—
The De'il could only work his perfect ill
   By leaving man without her !

Maye Cottage.

WHEN dreams of love first came to me,
  They pictured some secluded shade,
Where vines, and flowers, and birds should be ;
  And all the noisy world's parade
    A thrilling story told :
A story strangely grand, but vain,
  Remembered less and less,
While purer pride and pleasure reign,
  And day and night by turns impress
    Wise teachings manifold.

And now within my cottage home,
  The same I dreamed in early years,
I rest me, nor would further roam
  Along the crowded path of tears—
    The path that leads to death :
For only here may life be found ;
  'Tis smiling in the gentle flowers—
The birds are singing it around—
  'Tis glancing in the sunny showers—
    And all hath blesséd breath !

With her I love, to sit and read—
  With her I love, to calmly talk ;

Or, when the golden clouds succeed
    The sultry, breathless noon, to walk
        Beneath the quivering trees,
Silent awhile, or speaking now,
    While hand is fondly clasping hand,
Until the stars come out, and THOU,
    GOD of the promised Eden land,
        Art whispering in the breeze!

The stars are thick; I see the dew
    Like diamonds on the drooping grass:
The lamp will yet the day renew;—
And slow the winding way we pass,
        Where friends and song invite,
Or books, or prints of distant shore,
    Old castles, abbeys, pleasing scenes
Which all the ancient time restore,
    As fancy o'er the picture leans,
        With eyes of fairy light!

And still the dearest theme of all
    Is HOME—there is no other word
Which can, as by enchantment, call
    Around us flower, and breeze, and bird,
        And love, the soul of bliss!
O, sweetest word of mortal speech!
    O, worthy of an angel tongue!
Indeed dost thou to true-love teach
    A beauty never, never sung—
        A Home so dear as this!

Niagara.

WRITTEN AT THE FALLS, AUGUST 14TH, 1855.

NIAGARA!   My dream of many years—
This moment's living glory!
                    In my dream,
A beauty and a majesty, too fair,
Too grand, for music, poetry, or pencil :
Yet in reality !—
                    Why now attempt
The vast impossible !

                    I may describe
Thy height, thy depth ; measure thy rocky walls ;
Speak of thy snowy foam ; thy steam-like spray ;
The rainbow, spanning with its heaven-born grace
Thy multitudinous waters, white and emerald ;
Then may I turn unto thy varied shore,
Pile rocks on rocks, and crowd the tangled trees ;
Here scatter flowers ; and there the soft grass spread ;
And fill the islands with enchanting sounds
Of birds, and winds, and waves : but all in vain !
'Tis not Niagara ; or 'tis alone
To those who have beheld, as I behold ;
Those in whose minds the mighty memory lingers,
That memory that must remain forever !

Thou hast not seen the Wonderful?
                                For thee
Man can do little.   Do not trust his pen,
Nor trust his pencil more.   These are but outlines,
Feeble, unmeaning—save when thou hast seen !
Like stenographic characters, they give
Thoughts to him only who is in the secret.

Niagara ! with ever new delight,
Day after day, I gaze upon thy grandeur.
My soul is captive to thy god-like power,
And so all-sweet is such captivity,
That I would have the world thus bound with me !

Therefore, the pen and pencil, each in turn,
I grasp, to show the world thy majesty,
But, disappointed, soon resign them both,
And look, and listen, and am lost in GOD !

These words are merely spray-drops from the Falls,
Yet if, descending on old memories,
They serve to keep them green, and cheer the hope
In other hearts, till it shall grow, and bear
Reality's rich fruit—I am content.

Each for himself must see.   Niagara
Will do the rest: Filling thy soul with beauty,
Love, adoration !

                        Lo ! it springs from Heaven
Down to the tortured depths ! To Heaven again
Up-springs the thin and scattering cloud of mist,

Where the soft rainbow part reveals itself;
While myriad voices, shouts, and shrieks, and thunderings,
The tramp of armies————
The clash of arms, the rush of maddened steeds,
The trumpet call, the cry of victory,
Loud lamentation—strangely all unite—
As all Earth's discords shall be music yet!—
With organ-like expression of high thoughts,
Proclaiming: GOD! Most wonderful! Most wonderful!
GOD of Niagara! and GOD of Love!

Cottage Scene.

THE last few flowers are fading fast,
   That round my Cottage smiled,
I hear November's moaning blast,
   The clouds are dark and wild.

The trees, the music-making trees,
   That soothed my grassy rest,
When nature's dreamy harmonies
   Stole, hallowing, o'er my breast:

I see them from the lattice now,
   But few the leaves they bear,
Still clinging to the cheerless bough,
   Like Love to lone Despair.

Farewell the garden's winding ways!
   Its perfume-breathing bowers!

The beautiful, glad summer days!
  The pensive moonlit hours!

Let fall the curtain. Sad the night,
  But here is gloom forgot!
Blow on, ye winds!—my hearth is bright!
  Blow on! I fear ye not!

For books are mine, and friends are mine,
  And dear they be, though few;
And round my pleasant parlor shine
  Fair scenes I love to view.

Fair scenes that dread no wintry wind,
  Fond friends, from youth-time tried,
And grand old books, wherein I find
  Whate'er is good beside:—

Save love—Thou smilest, Maye! I'look
  For love, to thee alone;
Thy heart is yet my favorite book,
  Where joy is ever known!

What care I now, though sad the hour?
  Its gloom is here forgot!
Blow on, ye winds! exert your power!
  Blow on! I fear ye not!

And thus, when life is fading fast,
  And lowers the chilly night—
Be dark the clouds! and moan the blast!
  If all within be bright!
  11

Lazarus.

'Twas morn in Bethany, a summer morn,
And all its towers, and odoriferous groves,
Beamed in the golden sun.   A sound of harps,
With intermingled voice of joyous song,
Came sweetly forth from many a noble hall.
Even the weary slave was glad awhile,
Feeling upon his heart the cheerful light,
That imaged peace and dreams of other days!

Alas! the loveliness, and mirth, and pride
Of morn's enchanting hour, were mockery
To those who stood in silent sorrowing,
And thought of him—the loved—the early lost!

Mary was pale, and yet most beautiful,
Though grief had stolen many charms away.
Her dark, full eyes were dim and heavy now;
And fled the vermil tint, and circling form,
That gave her lip the grace of virgin youth.
                    Gay flowers no more adorned
Her ebon-braided hair, but now it fell
In wild confusion down her snowy neck.
And Martha's azure eyes were tearful, too,
Like violets in the rain.   Her auburn tresses
Half loosened waved around her heaving breast.

Well may the sisters weep, and stand apart,
And disregard the sympathy of friends,
The joyous light, the silver strain of harps,
And art's magnificence, and nature's pride,
Since Lazarus is dead—their brother dead !
O, he was kind and excellent of soul,
And lived in beauty, as the graceful palm,
Shading the arid sands, a shelter still,
And still a hope, where all beside is fear.

At last the SAVIOUR's near approach was known ;
And Martha went to meet him ; and anon
Mary arrived, and falling at his feet,
She cried, in all the bitterness of woe :
" Hadst THOU been here, my brother had not died !"

Tears from her eyes fell fast.   The Jews, who thronged
With friendship round the maid, though brave and stern,
And often tried in scenes of misery,
Gave answering tears of sorrow :—
                              "JESUS wept !"

It was a lone and rugged cave, wherein
The form of Lazarus in death reposed.
And o'er it waved a gloomy cypress tree,
And only tone of rustling leaves, and sweet
Funereal hymn of birds, were whispered there.
Even the flowers that bloomed above the grave,
With seeming consciousness of melancholy,
Looked down.
              " Take ye away the stone !"
                              'Twas done.

And JESUS raised his eyes to Heaven, communing,
By few and simple words of love and praise,
With GOD the FATHER; then he cried aloud:
" Lazarus, come forth !"
　　　　　　　　　And instantly he came !

No dream ! no dream ! he breathes—he moves—he lives !
And swift returns the roseal cheek of health,
And smile of tenderness, and early joy !
And bound the sisters to embrace their brother,
And kiss a welcome to the world again !

The Poetess.

BLOOMING like the virgin Spring;
Lips to smile, to kiss, and sing;
Eyes that softly, brightly roll,
Full of ecstacy of soul;
Cheeks where timid roses grow,
Stealing up through moon-lit snow;
Ringlets falling carelessly,
Dark as stormy night may be.

Forward, with a simple grace,
Bends the love-creating face,
Eagerly, as if to hear
Music of a distant sphere,

Blissful, high, immortal tone,
Only to the chosen known ;
Anxiously, as if to find
Angels in the Realm of Mind,
Gentle, bountiful, and bright,
Seen by inspiration's light !

Thus from mysteries above
Shall be woven songs of love,
Themes of gratitude and praise,
Which the lowly one shall raise,
Whisper peace, and teach the heart,
'T is of GOD and Heaven a part,
Till the pilgrim, Man, shall go
Singing through the Vale of Woe !

The Captive.

FROM THE FRENCH. AUTHOR UNKNOWN.

That pain is still a part of life, we know,
   Whatever sea or land we wander o'er,
But only feel the true and deepest woe
   When suffering, distant from our native shore !

And if, in silent night, a gentle sleep
   The beautiful and cherished scene restore,
    11*

The Captive's spirit only wakes to weep
   The vanished pleasures of his native shore!

When Fancy calls to life futurity,
   Ah, then he feels the present fate no more,
Till clanking chains excite a memory,
   That sad, sweet memory, his native shore!

If kindly words like sudden sunshine fall,
   And light the gloom that never smiled before,
His happy heart forgets the weary thrall—
   But—he is distant from his native shore!

The Warrior's Last Words.*

THE aged Chief, amid the city's pride,
   Weary and faint, with slow-consuming pain,
Now for his forest home and kindred sighed,
   For only one fond look, one word—in vain!

He felt the pitiless approach of death,
   And feebly called his grieving brothers near,
And spoke with solemn tone of failing breath,
   While o'er his lowly couch they bent to hear:

* PUSH-MA-TA-HA. He died at Washington, D. C., and was buried in the Congress Cemetery, where a monument has been erected to his memory.

"I now shall die, but you will journey back
    To join our friends, the whispering prairies o'er,
And flowers will bloom along the winding track,
    And birds will sing—for me, alas, no more!

"At last ye see your lodges' wreathing smoke,
    Ye come—'t is told—they gaze upon the ground;
'T is like the fall of some majestic oak,
    When silence reigns in all the woods around!"

Almost Home.

I am almost home!   I hear the bells!
What happiness their music tells!
What smiles and tones of long ago
Fill my heart, till its joys o'erflow!

I am almost home!   I see the tower!
And near it lies my own dear bower!
They are gazing far, they fondly wait,
E'en now, I know, at the garden gate!

I am almost home!   But who is this?
If it must be so, I will grant a kiss!
"One more?"   How strange these lovers be,
Asking one, and taking three!

Ottoa.

An erroneous idea generally prevails in regard to the poetical character of our aborigines. According to the fashionable novels and poems, one of these sentimental savages—

"cannot ope
His mouth, but out there flies a trope."

The following is a translation from a genuine Indian love song.

OTTOA 'mid the prairie flowers,
　　How beautiful the sight!
More handsome than a wampum belt,
　　And more than scarlet bright!
I 'll put my best blue leggings on,
　　And chase the charming maid,
And she will run away from me,
　　As if she were afraid!
　　　　　Ottoa! Ottoa! the laughing prairie flower!
　　　　　Ottoa! Ottoa! I seek thee for my bower!

But now she turns her head around,
　　To mock, and laugh, and rail,
And well I see 't is all pretence,
　　And Love will soon prevail!
The pretty *witcheannas* thus
　　The hearts of men beguile,
And if they frown and run away,
　　They stop again, and smile!
　　　　　Ottoa! Ottoa! the laughing prairie flower!
　　　　　Ottoa! Ottoa! I seek thee for my bower!

Emma.

Shall beauty be my theme of praise,
  When verse aspires to honor thee?
Ah no, for even as we gaze
  May beauty fade, and cease to be.
The loveliness whereon I look
  Shall not detain my soaring song;
Though fair the cover of a book,
  Within should praise or blame belong.
And I have read thy mind aright,
  And pleasure found in every page,
Anticipating new delight
  E'en to the winter-time of age :—
The winter-time?   Thy spirit's smile
Will make a summer all the while!

Youth and Love.

Dost thou remember when the night was late—
    I must, in sooth, correct my truant line,
For night no more, but morn, did dominate,
    Though still the moon and stars did feebly shine :—
Dost thou remember, near the rustling bower,
    When, silent now, and now conversing low,
Embracing, we reclined, and felt the power,
    The trust, the bliss, that youth and love bestow !
The world did seem a Paradise, in which
    Nor thought of fear, nor ill would dare intrude ;
And we in all its ecstacies were rich,
    In sacred love, and pensive solitude !
The morn grew brighter, then 't was grief to part :
Fly swiftly, Time ! and bind us heart to heart !

Zahara.

A dweller of the Desert,
A maiden wild and swift,
A laughing girl, and beautiful!

Her tent was by the well,
Beneath the shading palm;
An hour—it is not there,
But on the arid waste,
The wilderness of sand,
The hot and shining sand,
    Far, far away!
The unbroken plain around,
The unclouded sky above!

Upon a living throne,
A strange and lofty throne,
Swift as the wind she rode
Across the silent Desert!

Grandly the camel bore her:
Its long, ungainly neck
Extended, and its legs,
Its lank and sinewy legs,
Striding the conquered distance!

Even on the dewless sands,
Beneath the burning sun;
Even where no grass can grow—
The rose of love is blooming!
The pitying angels see,
And sprinkle it with tears;
Their claspéd hands, in prayer,
Avert the Day-God's wrath,
And shield it from his sight—
The delicate rose of love,
The rose that must not die!

Far from her father's tent—
Her guide the wreathing smoke:
A tall and widening column,
Whose capital was heaven:
Grandly the camel bore her.
Forward she bent, and gazed!
Patient, awhile, lone Arab youth!
Straight to thy heart she comes!

The sun is blotted out—
And the air is hot with death:
The terrible Simoon!

Not by the signal column,
Not on the wreck-strewn sand,
Not where the kiss of love may dread
The storm of hatred more—
And yet the lovers meet!

Vision of Battle.

'TWAS in my summer dreaming,
  Cool shaded 'neath a tree,
That all this wondrous seeming
  Came visiter to me.

I saw two armies meeting,
  Their broad, bright banners float:
Glad echo soft repeating
  Proud music's thrilling note!

And, crimson day declining,
  How all-enchanting fair,
Sword, spear, and helmet shining,
  With plumes wide waving there!

A pageant vast and splendid,
  Like some romantic dream!
As if from Heaven descended
  The Gods, in glory's beam!

*   *   *   *   *
*   *   *   *   *

I looked, and lo! a solemn,
  Dread change came over all;
12

For now, through every column,
  Each banner was a pall!

Each banner, black and stooping,
  Sword, helmet, spear, and plume!
Thus marched they, slow and drooping,
  Like mourners to a tomb!

The music ceased its cheering,
  Inebriating strain,
While loftily careering,
  And sounded not again!

As clouds, the tempest over,
  When spent their lightning wrath,
Move feebly back, and hover,
  Confused, along their path:

Thus, gloomily and broken,
  Retiring ere they met,
The armies: and, a token
  Of peace, the fair sun set.

'Twas in my summer dreaming,
  Cool shaded 'neath a tree,
That all this wondrous seeming
  Came visiter to me.

Yet thought I after: Truly,
  If battle's glittering show
Were reft away, and duly
  Replaced by garb of woe:

If music ceased its magic, ·
   Fierce maddening every breast,
Then history were less tragic,
   The dove were then our crest!

'Twas in my summer dreaming,
   Cool shaded 'neath a tree,
That all this wondrous seeming
   Came visiter to me.

The Poet.

THERE was a poor youth, with a very girlish look,
   And yet was it sad to see,
For he read so much in an old, old book,
   And strange, wild thoughts had he!
        Away with the book and the pen!
        And out with the crowds of men!
        You wear away your body and soul,
        And what's your reward, Boy, then?

He looked on the World with his large, dark eyes;
   They rolled with a sovereign pride:
Then was he humble, and then came sighs;
   But not with a word he replied.
        Away with the book and the pen!

Yet he was not always, always sad :
  In the golden summer days,
Alone in the fields, would a flower make him glad,
  Or the wild bird's sweet, shrill lays !
      Away with the book and the pen !

In the green, soft shade, by the willowy stream,
  Would he write his music-thought,
Till, through the clouds, his happy dream
  The wings of angels caught !
      Away with the book and the pen !

They found him sleeping 'mid the flowers,
  A smile on his pale, cold face ;
But his soul, in a fairer Land than ours,
  No mortal eye may trace !
      Away with the book and the pen !

He had walked the earth : they knew him not :
  He went to the angel shore :
Yet never here shall his name be forgot,
  And his loving, blissful lore !
      For the book and the sacred pen,
      They have made him dear to men ;
      And beauty and truth now offer the world
      The joy that he dreamed of then !

The Bird at the Helm.

"The captain of the Norwegian barque Ellen states that when he was twenty miles distant from the Central America, a bird appeared on his vessel, and three times flew in his face, which caused him to change his course two points, and thus he came to the ill-fated steamer."—*Incidents of the wreck of the Central America.*

A bird came out on the stormy sea:
I stood at the helm—it came to me;
Thrice it flew in my face, and then
Flew away in the storm again.
  What did the bird of the stormy sea—
  What did the bird portend to me?

I stood at the helm—the strange bird crost—
It struck me, and two points I lost;
In her new course my bark must go,
For the strange, strange bird would have it so!
  What did the bird of the stormy sea,
  The spirit bird, portend to me?

Over the deep was darkest night,
Blackness all—then awful light—
Rush of waves and thunder roll:
I stood in the storm and said to my soul:
  What did the bird of the shrieking sea,
  The ghost-like bird, portend to me!
12*

Norway's rocks are bleak and bare;
But if no more I rest me there!
And if no more—My soul leaped up
And dashed in the night my sorrow's cup :—
    Lo ! what the bird of the stormy sea,
    The Heaven-sent bird, portends to thee.

O God ! that moment, before my bark,
Tossed on the billows deep and dark,
Hundreds, hundreds of dying men !—
Let me not see such sight again !
    This, O bird of the stormy sea,
    This didst thou portend to me !

*   *   *   *   *   *   *

Yet, by Him who sent thee, bird,
Shall ever the praise of my soul be heard,
That many were saved who, but for thee,
Had gone to the grave of the secret sea.
    For this, dear bird of the ravenous sea,
    I thank thy Guide, who guided me !

And the Dove, that still in life's unrest,
He sends with peace from His loving breast,
May it find us, whithersoe'er we roam,
And singing of Heaven, conduct us home !
    Bird of the Blest, life's stormy sea,
    From its deep despair, calls up to thee.

The Doomed City.

In a far-off verdant valley,
  Savage mountains round it,
By a Great Salt Lake, a City,
    Strangely built, and strangely peopled,
    Like a Christian City steepled,
Rises.—Who has found it?

To the Red Tribes is it known,
  To the tribes of lance and bow,
To the fleet deer is it known,
  And the headlong buffalo :
These have looked upon it, passing,
  These have seen with wondering eyes,
Then away among the mountains,
Through the forest, o'er the prairies,
  Swept with their surprise !

In the wilderness, a City :
Yet the world, with love or pity,
  All the world has heard its name :
Some have heard it, and received it,
As a sacred thing believed it,
And, with pilgrim-like devotion,
  Day and night, and day and night,
O'er the hills and vales of ocean,
  Journeyed to the Latter Light.

Others, when they heard the story,
Saw the tinsel of the glory,
Saw the strange deceit, the madness,
Saw the end that was not yet.

*   *   *   *   *

All the while the City numbered,
    Day by day, its pilgrims more;
All who came within it slumbered,
By a wondrous magic cumbered,
    Dreaming dreams of Earth-Heaven o'er.
Unto them came GOD in dreams,
    Angels, prophets, came to them,
With a promise—thus it seems—
    Of the whole world's diadem!
All should yet be theirs : each nation
    'Neath their hot hands melt like snow;
But with them was true salvation;
    They the triumph-trump should blow.

Women heard them—to their wiles
Gave the witchery of their smiles,
    Hearts and hands on them bestowing,
For 't was thus, and thus alone,
Should the heavenly bliss be known,
And gained the universal throne—
    Such the revelation's showing.

Now it was the reign of lust,
    And the reign of law was done :
'Why should GOD's own falchion rust?
    Draw the steel, and all is won !'

'Treason!' on Pacific's shore,
  'Treason!' by Atlantic tide,
Rose, and met.   And rose and met
    Men with souls of hero pride,
    Men in truth's great battle tried,
O'er whose memories the past
A halo-light of glory cast,
    Promising new glory yet.

In the far-off Mormon valley,
    Solitude claimed every home;
Those who dwelt therein departed,
Broken-hearted—broken-hearted—
    Whither shall they roam?

Like an exhalation, Error
    Flames along the startled sky;
Look, but do not look in terror—
    'Tis decreed to flash and die.

Love Song.

RECLINING on the grassy ground,
With checkered shade of trees around,
And song of birds, and bloom of flowers,
I dream away the golden hours,
And think of all that's dear to me,
Of youth and beauty, love and thee!

And thus my thoughts in music flow,
With tones of pleasure, soft and low;
They rise at first from nature's pride,
But soon to sweeter themes they glide,
And dwell content where Love displays
Thy youthful charms, thy winning ways!

And still a dearer joy for me
Hath nature blent with thoughts of thee,
As Eden's bliss was only crowned
When Eve's angelic smile was found;
And heart and eyes, once cold and blind,
Now warmly welcome all mankind!

December.

THE wind is sighing,
The snow deep lying,
With crisp ice covered,
 On the frozen ground,

No sky appearing,
No sunbeam cheering,
But pale clouds rolling,
 Rolling round.

The tall trees shiver,
By the creaking river,
Where oft the icicles
    Shrilly fall,

From cliffs o'erbending,
From boughs descending,
With snow full-laden,
    Leafless all.

'T is gloomier growing;
The wind is blowing
Stronger, louder,
    Through the night.

A blank of sadness:
Yet, for gladness
Seeks my spirit—
    Lo! 't is light!

The fire is burning,
The taper turning
The fearful darkness
    Back to day.

Books surround me;
Joy hath found me;
Drear December
    Steals away.

Come Home.

"Where should this music be? i' the air, the earth?"

Tempest.

WHERE'ER in foreign clime
    We sadly stray
A gentle spirit glides
    Across our way,
And softly whispers: 'Cease, O cease to roam!
Love calls thee through her tears: Come Home! Come
    Home!'

There is a voice that dwells
    In every breeze,
In mossy sylvan cells,
    And trembling trees,
A voice forever heard, where'er we roam,
With Ariel's music charm: 'Come Home! Come Home!'

'Come Home! Thy lonely friends
    In silence see
The old familiar haunts,
    So dear to thee
When happy youth had never dreamed to roam
From Love's bright Paradise: Come Home! Come Home!'

When life's last lingering ray
Begins to fade,
Not desolate shall be
The gathering shade;
Then sweet from Heaven the voice : 'No longer roam;
Come to the Home of Bliss!   Come Home! Come Home!'

The Poet's Soul.

A Poet's Soul hath sovereignty
    O'er every Soul of Earth,
Hath still the noblest destiny,
    By God-appointed birth,
And worldly rank to it shall be
    Of unconsidered worth ;
For Heaven hath crowned it lord of all,
And throned it, that it may not fall!

A Poet's Soul the angels teach,
    With glad immortal lyre,
Endow it with divinest speech,
    And ever-living fire :
A voice that every heart shall reach,
    A flame that shall inspire,
Till all who prove the voice and flame,
Shall worship Him from whom they came !
    13

Bladensburg.

"THE TIME THAT TRIED MEN'S SOLES."

IT was at ancient Bladensburg,
  The weather wondrous hot;
And motionless the tall corn stood,
  In every garden lot:
And in the shade, supinely laid,
  Cats, dogs, and pigs were seen;
And geese went sailing on the brook,
  Where drooped the willows green:

Went sailing forth as pleasantly
  As nothing were the matter!
Each praising her reflected charms,
  In most delightful clatter.
They little thought the hour was fraught
  With direful charge of ill,
That fast the angry Red-Coats came,
  Both geese and men to kill!

Sad sight to see as e'er could be,
  The white-washed village Inn,
With none to smoke, and none to joke,
  And none to sit and grin!
Now on the counter of the bar
  Half-emptied was the can;
The whiskey-tap neglected stood;
  To waste the liquor ran!

For fat and jolly John, the host,
   Had ta'en his rusty gun,
And so had Sam, the stable-boy,
   And every mother's son;
And out they went, with brave intent,
   To meet the coming foe,
To strike for ancient Bladensburg,
   And lay the tyrant low!

Still, sometimes here would child appear,
   Sage matron, buxom maid,
Crossing in haste the sandy street,
   Or whispering, sore afraid;
And busily preparing all
   To leave the luckless village,
Their corn and pigs, their ducks and geese,
   To fire, and sword, and pillage!

And up the bold militia marched,
   From town and country round;
The mighty men of Washington
   Came also to the ground :
For higher prize allured the eyes
   Of England's martial host,
Than Bladensburg, with all its wealth
   And old renown, could boast!

"The Capital!   The Capital!"
   Was still the foeman's cry.
Who for his Nation's Capital
   Would not with pleasure die?
And so they swore to fall, before
   The foeman should prevail,

And pile the field with Britishers,
  Beneath their hissing hail!

Hence, hither, too, our Regulars
  Assembled for the fight;
And gay-plumed Volunteers—O, Mars!
  A grand, terrific sight!
And on his steed, to do or bleed,
  Our President was here:
And every man did shout "Hurra!"
  And not a soul did fear!

A cloud of dust flew down the street—
  A horse and rider in it:—
'Twas rather warm to run a race,
  But surely he would win it!
Cats, pigs did leap from out their sleep,
  And dogs did bark amain,
And children cried, and women screamed,
  And geese confessed their pain!

But on the furious horseman rushed,
  A soldier, minus hat;
The streams of heat abundant gushed—
  He did n't stop for that!
"They're coming!" was his only word,
  Hoarse, choked with dust: "they're coming!"
And on he passed to where, right fast,
  Was heard a distant drumming.

He gained the Yankee lines, and shrieked
  "They're coming!"—as he fell!

They took him up, with instant care,
  And begged him further tell—
But vainly: though with brandy plied,
  No other word he spoke
Save "Coming! Coming!"—while the drumming
  Loud and louder woke!

At length, along the turnpike-road,
  The Red-Coats came, indeed:
They reached the little bridge, but there
  We checked their daring speed.
Whene'er they tried, we swept aside
  Their ranks with cannon-ball:—
Till pity spread throughout our troops,
  To see so many fall!

In mercy, we resolved to run,
  Yet were we not afraid;
And lest our noble action should
  Unkindly be repaid,
We left the bloody field, and sought
  The deep and tangled wood,
Where every man in such course ran
  As to himself seemed good.

The Battle of old Bladensburg!
  A scene of honest glory!
Though little of our true desert
  Is given us in story.
They say, our Capital was lost,
  Because we would not fight!
Is mercy, then, no grace in men,
  Unless they 're gainers by 't?
13*

The Smoker.

I saw him after dinner,
  And his face was like the sun,
When wearily he goes to rest,
  His long day's journey done.
The beef had made it hot,
  And the wine had made it red,
And a cloud was all around it,
  Like a curtain round a bed.

His chair was tilted back,
  And his feet were on the wall,
And the sorrows of the world
  Did not trouble him at all !
For though he toiled and puffed,
  Like an engine, or a stove,
Yet smiled amid his labors
  This " cloud-compelling Jove !"

Again I passed his dwelling,
  In the darkness of the night;
And still I knew the Smoker,
  Like a glow-worm, by his light.
His head was still thrown back,
  And his feet were still on high,
And he had a most peculiar look
  From out his half-shut eye.

'Twas morning; and I saw him,
  This great Vesuvius man,
And o'er the news-full paper
  His misty vision ran;
For still the fire was there,
  And still the smoke was thick:
And I remembered me the tales
  Whose hero was—Old Nick!

I wondered, if he slept?
  Or ever went about?
Or was he only some machine?
  For what?   Ah, there's the doubt!
Though puffing, always puffing,
  He never seemed to go:
What good he did by staying there,
  Is more than yet I know.

A beggar-boy craved charity.
  The Smoker "blessed his stars!"
And said, "he had no change to spare"—
  Then sent for more cigars!
The patient wife at last complains;
  He gruffly bids her cease:
" My home's a hell: it's very hard
  I cannot *smoke* in peace!"

Yankee Doodle.

YANKEE Doodle! long ago
  They played it to deride us,
But now we march to victory,
  And *that's* the tune to guide us!
    Yankee Doodle! ha! ha! ha!
    Yankee Doodle Dandy!
    How we made the Red-Coats run
    At Yankee Doodle Dandy!

To fight is not a pleasant game,
  But if we must—we'll *do it!*
When " Yankee Doodle" once begins,
  The Yankee boys go through it!
    Yankee Doodle! ha! ha! ha!
    Yankee Doodle Dandy!
    " Go ahead !" our captains cry,
    At Yankee Doodle Dandy!

And let her come upon the sea,
  The insolent invader,
There our Yankee boys will be,
  Prepared to serenade her!
    Yankee Doodle! ha! ha! ha!
    Yankee Doodle Dandy!
    Yankee guns will sing the bass
    Of Yankee Doodle Dandy!

Yankee Doodle! How it brings
  The good old days before us!
Two or three began the song—
  Millions join the chorus!
     Yankee Doodle! ha! ha! ha!
     Yankee Doodle Dandy!
    Rolling round the continent
     Is Yankee Doodle Dandy!

Yankee Doodle! Not alone
  The continent will hear it,
But every land shall catch the tone,
  And every tyrant fear it!
     Yankee Doodle! ha! ha! ha!
     Yankee Doodle Dandy!
    Freedom's voice is in the song
     Of Yankee Doodle Dandy!

Here and Hereafter.

DEATH's desolation daily moveth on :
  The cottage rose, how fair its early bloom!
A moment, and the simple joy is gone,
  Darkened forever in the lonely tomb.

Splendor, and song, and thrilling music tone,
  Casting enchantment o'er the palace hall :

A moment, these delights are strangely flown,
  Silence and sorrow dispossessing all !

Why bid the mourner dry his gushing tears ?
  Why not relieve the overflowing heart ?
The form where clung so many hopes and fears,
  Shall it with cold indifference depart ?

No ! still affection shall the tribute pay,
  The parting tears shall fully, freely flow :
Yet blissful visions to the soul shall say :
  " Remember ! this is not eternal woe !"

Only a night of absence—'tis no more ;
  How beautiful will be the promised morn !
The lost of earth will Heaven more bright restore,
  The dead, ev'n while we weep, again are born !

Where ? in what starry world of yonder sky ?
  What destiny shall linger with them there ?
Shall they in joy live evermore ?—or die,
  To live again in some still brighter sphere ?

Thus on, and on, from world to higher world,
  In each receiving still-increasing good,
Till God's own glory slowly be unfurled,
  Till all His power, His love be understood !

" Our Father !" Thou hast taught us that dear name !
  We move in darkness, yet we trust to Thee !
Believing, in the Land from whence we came,
  We shall again Thy happy children be !

The Last Night of Summer.

AFAR the Moon, in maiden majesty,
   Pursues her azure path, and softly bright
   The timid stars impart their changing light.
'Tis now the noon of silence; now for me
There seems a charm around, above, to be;
   So holy is the stillness of the night,
   So beautiful whate'er my roving sight
On hill, and dale, and winding stream may see!
   A passing breeze sighs o'er me; from afar
Comes a fond strain, a plaintive whisper tone,
   Uniting with the voice of deep guitar,
That tells of lover's joy, and lover's moan.
Thus the Last Night of Summer glides along,
With moon and star-beam, music, love and song!

Hours at Home.

God bless thee, Maye! This sultry afternoon,
　　Weary and sad of thought, I cast me down,
Resting, but sleeping not: so kind a boon
　　Then hopeless. Like a poor, beleaguered town,
Within my heart was sorrow meeting sorrow,
And none that ever dreamed of brighter morrow.

I closed mine eyes. Now softly through the room
　　I heard the careful steps of her I love;
And presently there spread a pleasant gloom
　　Around me, for the sun shone bright above,
Too bright for slumber. Presently I knew
She stood, and gazed, and watched each breath I drew.

Then stole away so tenderly—one look,
　　A long and sweet one, as she passed the door,
Escaping with her newly-opened book,
　　Her slow steps mounting to our chamber floor.
Of this a part I saw, and felt a part,
For love observeth, even from the heart!

Over my sorrows came the smile of peace,
　　As over stormy waves the sunset ray,
Till, less and less disturbed, at last they cease,
　　And calmly mirror back the golden day.

Over the deluge of my soul came love,
Bearing an olive-branch, like Noah's dove.

And then I fancied brighter time, and then
   Distinctly rose a vine-clad cottage wall,
Far down the forest winding of a glen,
   And near the tinkling of a waterfall;
And this was all mine own, and she was here,
Making my happy state, O doubly dear!

And friends were mine, good friends, though only few,
   Who shared, in summer days, my fragrant bower,
Or by my social hearth, in winter, drew,
   While verse and story sped the pensive hour.
Not far the city lay: at Sabbath time,
Over the hills, we heard the church-bells chime!

What merry parties on the grassy plain!
   What rambling rides among the bending trees!
Often with friends, but oft, and oft again,
   Only dear MAYE and I; the perfumed breeze
Waving her auburn curls, as, gladsomely,
Her proud steed bounded on, so wild and free!

On sprang our steeds, through sun and checkered shade,
   Down the green vale and up the gentle hill,
Or instantly, in full career, obeyed,
   And stood with arching necks, waiting our will!
Dismounting, then we rested by a spring,
Drank the cool tide, and heard the linnet sing:

And watched the broad oak leaves that whirling fell;
   And through the forest vista looked afar,
  14

Talked quietly, and, loving all things well,
    Came slowly homeward 'neath the evening star:
To pass, perchance, the early hours of night
With books that made the very darkness light!

We lived not for ourselves alone : we taught
    Whate'er of wisdom and of good we knew,
And our reward was—only this we sought—
    The grateful smile that often met our view,
The consciousness that children loved us more,
And old men, entering, blessed our cottage door!

In the lone forest sometimes would I stray,
    And 'mid the inspirations breathing there,
Would let my thoughts pursue their music way,
    Singing of all things bountiful and fair;
Trusting they should exist, and oft be read,
When he who wrote them slumbered with the dead.

Again, when desolate the wintry scene,
    In the small book-room would we sit together,
Where some sweet page preserved our own world green,
    Enchanting it beyond all gloomy weather:
Or, also there, would come the lightsome rhyme,
With which our hearts, forever young, kept time!

And this—I know not how it was—was now;
    We were not old, but looking forward yet
Right trustfully, with calm, exalted brow,
    To many joys, before our sun should set,
Nor fearing loss of all, when sank that light:
Do not the stars shine out to bless the night?

Such were my fancies, and the sweetest still
  Were those that pictured her confiding soul,
Faithful and kind, confronting every ill;
  And, where her tenderness could not control,
Soothing and cheering, by her angel love,
Parting the cloud, revealing Heaven above !

Her smiling face !—I woke !   It was before me,
  Smiling as I beheld it in my sleep :
And as so lovingly 't was bending o'er me,
  I gazed, I smiled ; then could not choose but weep.
My strength returned, the storm that darkly lowered
Rolled back, by Love's omnipotence o'erpowered !

Ramble by the River.

At summer evening's roseal hour,
  When care and toil were o'er,
I wandered, lone and pensively,
  Potomac's shining shore.
It was a sweet and quiet scene,
  To woo the pencil's art,
And with inexplicable joy
  O'erflow the poet's heart !

Around my winding, pebbly path
    Was solitude supreme,
Save now and then a truant bird,
    That glanced across the stream,
And near or far, where'er it went,
    With wing as swift and light,
Its shadow, like a loving mate,
    Companion of its flight!

All silence, save the timid waves,
    That like a vestal train
To music sad and low advanced,
    Retired, and came again;
Save whispers by the rugged banks,
    And through the bending trees,
The gratitude of Earth to Heaven,
    The welcome of the breeze!

The forest-hills were purple-robed,
    And charmed the smiling eye
To where the tints evanished soft
    Along the mellow sky.
The fowler's lurking boat was seen,
    Quiescent, far away,
And here and there a graceful sail,
    Glad in the glowing day!

Now dim adown the dale appeared
    The City of my home,
But nobly yet and brightly rose
    Fair Freedom's sacred Dome,*

* The Capitol at Washington.

O ever thus, when night is near,
  May Heaven its smile bestow,
And all the glory beaming here,
  In distant bosoms glow!

The crescent moon, a lonely star,
  Adorn the darkening west,
And golden tints to silver pale,
  On sad Potomac's breast.
I linger long—but where is he,
  So dull of heart and cold,
Whom Nature's gentlest scenery,
  Whom Thought, have ne'er controlled?

Potomac hath but simple grace,
  But humble hills and vales;
No castles rising gloomily,
  No wild, chivalric tales;
And yet it is a storied scene,
  And here the true and brave
Will seek the home of WASHINGTON,
  And muse above his grave!

14*

The Wife o' "Kirkwood Hame."

My hills are green, an' crowned wi' trees,
    An' vines an' flowers are there,
An' o'er my vales the simmer breeze
    Wide waves the harvest fair.
I hear the bonnie birdies sing,
    An' I could sing the same,
Wi' thought o' her, the winsome thing,
    The Wife o' Kirkwood Hame!

I wad na gie my simple state
    For a' the warld hae seen,
I ask na ither gift o' fate
    Than ingle joy wi' Jean!
My cannie wee-ones by my side,
    Wha lisp their daddie's name,
As cheerfu' looks, wi' mither pride,
    The Wife o' Kirkwood Hame!

I 've mingled wi' the strife o' town,
    To trust, an' be deceived,
I felt my spirit drooping down,
    For meickle was it grieved:
But now, frae ilka ill awa',
    These cares my duty claim,
An' sweetly smiles aboon them a'
    The Wife o' Kirkwood Hame!

Sacred Love.

O Love! the fairest, dearest child thou art
  Of HIM who rules the myriad worlds of space;
In Heaven thy home is on HIS happy heart,
  And Earth receives with joy thy smiling face.
Beautiful Spirit! unto thee belong
  Wondrous enchantments never known before;
O the sweet charm that animates thy song!
  O the ineffable angelic lore
Thy presence breathes, of peace, and faith, and truth,
  Yet all with mystery, to win the soul,
And train by slow degrees its erring youth
  To gain the golden prize of Virtue's goal!
Thus, a bright visitant from Heaven is Love,
Whereof she whispers part, and offers all above!

The Indian Mound.*

'T WAS night, the noon of summer night,
And shone the stars serenely bright,
And from the silent homes of men
Alone I slowly wandered then,
                    Afar and pensively.

The joyous moon up-rose at last,
And o'er the river, gliding fast,
And o'er the plain, and tangled brake,
The hill, the dale, and quiet lake,
                    Her smile fell silvery!

Ah! sweet at such an hour to rove,
When earth around, and heaven above,
E'en in their very silence tell
The heart such tales as please it well,
                    Of love's futurity!

The Indian Mound! O, sacred place!
Proud tomb of a departed race!
How Fancy calleth back again
The crowd that moveth o'er the plain,
                    So slow, so mournfully!

* Near St. Louis, Missouri.

The chieftain dead they bear along—
The fitful wail—the burial song—
And prayers that would the lost recall—
And tears that for the valiant fall,
        Who sleepeth placidly!

The many disappear, but yet,
Matoa! *thou* canst not forget—
Thou canst not, though his eyes be dim,
And cold his heart, depart from him,
        Once loved so tenderly!

Tomb of the gentle, wise, and brave!
Pride, worth, ambition's honored grave!—
Their very names have passed away,
And as the night doth conquer day,
        They faded presently!

And thus, perchance a little while,
When Death may steal the sunny smile,
The stranger passing by shall find
My grave—but only summer's wind
        To tell my history.

Alas, its ever-sighing tone,
Its *whence* and *whither* both unknown,
Its roving life, and nature frail,
Tell, truly tell, the tearful tale
        Of human destiny!

A Secret.

It was a most unnatural condition,
And bore too heavy on the lady's heart,
Which panted, struggled, moaned despairingly,
E'en as a carrier-bird, that longs to give
Its message, caring not who taketh it,
So anxious for relief.   The fair Matilda
Possessed a Secret, 't was important, too,
In sooth the most important maid can have,
Because relating to herself and John,
The dear John Smith, her bosom's destined lord.

They were " engaged," and long deliberation
Had fixed the happy day ; but John requested,
Moved by timidity, perhaps, or caution,
That none should know the contract.   She was willing,
At least she thought so then, yet Time revealed
Her heart with other wishes :—John controlled them,
For oft the lovers met, and every meeting
He urged the old request.   But now there came,
Throughout the District of the plighted pair,
A scarcity of cash, and not a house,
Either of delicate frame or ruddy brick,
Not e'en a shed, for coal, or cow, or horse,
Was seen uprising ; so our carpenter—
I should have told his trade some ten lines back—
One morning took the cars for Baltimore,

In search of work.   He had been gone a month,
And all that weary while had only written
Six letters to Matilda!   O 't was cruel!
What wonder that her gentle heart was sad?
What wonder such unfrequent intercourse
With him she loved should leave an aching void
In her affections?   Is it, then, surprising,
Thus overwhelmed with agony of absence,
She should assume her bonnet, muff, and shawl,
And, after seeing that the fire was safe,
Depart at once, with step of resolution,
Nor pause until she reached Miss Jackson's door,
Her nearest friend, and trust to Mary's bosom
The precious secret pining in her own?
The heart that once hath felt the blaze of love,
If chance should e'er withdraw the sacred torch,
Will in its lonely darkness surely languish,
Unless the light of friendship, though a taper,
With sympathy shine o'er its desolation.
Matilda told the tale, and Mary heard
With eager ears, and oft-repeated vows
Of lasting faith; and promised, as reward,
Her private parleys with the little god,
If e'er she met him.
                        Now, 't was wondrous sweet,
As both together on the sofa sat,
Or half reclined, with fair soft arms embraced,
And glossy curls that touched each other's cheek,
While cracked and sparkled cheerily the fire,
While puss with puzzled paws pursued her tail—
'T was sweet to see them, like a pair of sisters,
Mingle, in voice subdued, their angel souls!

Matilda felt how excellent is friendship,
And even dared to think that John himself
Could scarce make happier hour!   And then she rose,
Gave Mary. charge of sacred secrecy,
Replied in full to—"Tilda, why so soon?"
Repeated through the hall the parlor charge,
Once more, upon the porch—and sailed away.

The night was near, and Mary hurried off
To deck her beauty—Mrs. Lackingwit
Received to-night a chosen company.
A crowd was there, and Mary smiled around.
The poor piano heaved unnoticed groans,
And now and then a sentimental song
Was heard above the din of many tongues,
In music's hopeless horror :—then a pause,
As when a pedagogue alarms his school,
Deep, dreadful, breathless silence.
                                   " Mary, dear!"—
It was the very skeleton of sound,
Sharp, cold, and startling; 't was the ancient voice
Of Miss Almira Long, the awe of men,
The virgins' monitress, and scold of cooks :—
   " What color have you chosen for your bonnet?
I saw Matilda Jenks before your door
This afternoon, and hence I guess, my love,
You sent for her, to have a consultation."
   " No, Miss, it only was a friendly visit."
   " A visit, love! so, then, you are acquainted?"
   " Why not, Miss Long?"   "O nothing, nothing, love!
She is, no doubt, a good, well-meaning creature,
But dresses—though I 'm sure 't is not my business—

Above her station.   Why, a milliner
Should learn she 's not a lady; yes, she should :
And not be flirting out with muffs and plumes,
And taking to herself the Avenue !
Good gracious me ! I do declare ! I never !
But she 'll discover very few believe
'Fine feathers make fine birds'—she will, indeed !
And all her arts will never catch a husband !"
   "Her *arts*, Miss Long ?" the angry Mary cried,
"Now I can tell you, Tilda has *no* arts;
But if she wished a *teacher*, I could find one !
A husband, too !   Well, I can tell you, Miss,
Tilda could marry *now*, that 's more than *some* could,
For she 's engaged to Mr. Smith, of Georgetown,—
SHE TOLD ME SO TO-DAY !"
                         Miss Long was hushed ;
And silent wonder stared throughout the room.

Then Mary bound them all to keep the Secret :—
Ten ladies told my wife, the morning after,
My wife, *of course*, told me—*but here it ends !*

15

Time.

THE Spirit loves to wander back
　　The old, familiar past,
Or seek the future's wilderness,
　　Strange, visionary, vast!

But seldom will it rest its wing
　　Amid the present scene,
Though Pleasure wave her jewelled wand,
　　And Beauty smile, a Queen!

O Spirit! chain thy roving thought!
　　To-day alone is thine!
The star that lit thy early flight
　　Is doomed no more to shine!

But see! the glorious present hour
　　Reveals a nobler fate!
Come, win the Heaven-presented prize,
　　While sister Angels wait!

Act now! the future lures afar,
　　It may not smile for thee!
Yet shall thy deeds, or idleness,
　　A curse or blessing be!

Yes, millions, round the rolling World,
　　Thy life's effect shall know,

And teach the millions *after them*,
   Till countless ages flow!

Awake! thou knowest not thyself!
   Thy dignity behold!
Thy actions, good or ill, *must live!*
   Thy thoughts in Heaven are told!

Love's Lament.

I may never see thee more,
   Yet in each familiar place
Must I linger as before,
   And our timid love retrace:
As a spirit haunts the home
   Where it dwelt in mortal years,
With my solemn thoughts I roam,
   With my secret sighs and tears!

I may never see thee more;
   Though the world is dark to me,
Yet the past I'll not deplore,
   But I'll fondly think of thee,
Till the lesson of thy life,
   And the beauty of thy love,
Arch a rainbow o'er the strife,
   For my soul to thine above!

Evelene.

ESCAPED the city's dust and noise,
Its crime, and pride, and tinsel toys,
   I found a green, romantic hill,
Where vines and flowers were cheerful things,
And butterflies, with glorious wings,
   Were flitting at their own wild will;
And came the cedar-scented breeze,
Soft rustling through the grand oak trees.

O, sweet it was to fly from men,
To think—to read—and idly then,
   Perchance beneath the changing shade
On that far-seeing hill reclined,
Or where the murmuring waters wind
   Lovely and lone along the glade,
Idly, and yet with busy brain,
To woo and win the poet's train!

There is—there is—I care not how
The wise, with all-pretending brow,
   May mock and scorn my simple speech—
There is an inspiration taught
By scenes our BLESSED GOD hath wrought,
   A power, a bliss no man may teach!
And I have felt the sacred ray,
Which yet my words cannot portray.

But still it aids the striving soul
To comprehend its Lord's control,
   Thus breathing from the varied scene,
If happily there chance to be
Another in the mystery—
   Like mine with that of Evelene,
And higher truth the two may find
On Earth and in the Realm of Mind.

Fair friend, so lately known, yet well;
I prize, beyond my verse to tell,
   My spirit's intercourse with thine,
And like thy gift of sister love,
When lone I mused in yonder grove—
   A flower-wreathed bowl of fragrant wine—
So sweet thy cup of life be found,
With God's bright buds of promise round!

Pencil Marks in a Book.

Through all this summer morning I've been reading
The large, quaint pages of an olden story;
A book in which I've found a name unknown,
The name of some one who possessed it once,
Written in school-girl style, inclining down,
Most liberal of flourishes: " Her Book"
Beneath the signature; and then the date:
One hundred years ago!
   15*

                        I looked upon it
Often and long before I read the story,
Thinking, but vainly, ever, " Who was *she?*
Where dwelt the little maiden ?—whom she loved ?
And was she loved again ?   And was she happy ?—
And children, too, were hers, who read this book,
Smiling as she had smiled in early years ?
Then age arrived, perhaps ; and death at last—
Yes, surely death :" and thus my mind went on,
Striving in dreamy mood to trace the past,
Of which the simple fact of life gone out
Alone was manifest.

                        I conned each letter,
To learn some secret of her character,
For thus our modern sages say we can—
But rested still in doubt : then turned away,
And read and read the old, romantic page,
Finding full often in my pleasant course
Slight pencil marks along the ample margin,
And here and there some passage doubly marked,
And presently a word of admiration,
Or one or two dissenting.
                        Now no more
The name appeared unknown to me ; a friend
The stranger seemed ; her history familiar ;
For sympathy had brought our lives together
In a sweet unison : we smiled, we wept,
We hoped and feared together.   And the book
Had a new charm for me, beyond the story,
For her soft eyes first glanced along the lines,
For her kind heart was centred here awhile,
For her fair fingers wrote these loving words !

The Artist.

THE eve, when they bore thee all sadly away,
With the pride of the Summer was lovely and gay.
A storm had passed over the landscape, but now
The sunset fell soft on the gem-laden bough,
And the hills and the vales in their glory were dressed,
And purple and gold were the clouds of the west,
And the rainbow was up, and the beautiful birds
Beneath its grand arch sang their mystical words,
Like spirits of Heaven, ascended and sang,
Till fainter and fainter the melody rang.

They bore thee all sadly away to the tomb;
A death-cloud had darkened thy summer of bloom:—
The changes of nature, or wild or serene,
Thou had'st stood in the rapture of genius, and seen,
Seen by the light of beauty and love,
Which the BLESSED bestows from its fountain above,
That HIS chosen may teach to the children of Earth
The joys of their home, and the bliss of their birth !

Right nobly performed was thy mission divine,
As a wand was thy pencil, and all things were thine:
Glowing with freshness, and perfect in truth,
The landscape immortal lived on in its youth.
And yet in far time shalt thou please and inspire,
And awake in the soul a sweet love and desire,

A love that is holy, that lingers to gaze,
A hope that looks upward with prayer and with praise!

Thou art gone : and the passion that shone in thine eye,
And the skill of thy hand—dark and moveless they lie.
But I know it had pleased thy pure spirit to dream
Thou would'st pass to thy rest 'neath the sunset's glad
        beam,
When floated sublime, in their roseal hue,
The multiform clouds through the infinite blue,
When the rainbow stole out, when the birds were in
        song,
When the gold, slanting light, all the landscape along,
Was lovely and loving:—for thus did thine art
A glow and a beauty most fondly impart;
And gentle and warm as the sunset wert thou,
And thy last look a blessing, as evening's is now!

The Willow.

GENTLE Willow, now to thee
Shall my verse of praising be :
Fair thou art, exceedingly!

Oftentimes, in early lays,
Other trees had prouder praise,
In my forest-roving days :

Then I had not seen the Maid,
Who the meed of merit paid
Thee, beneath thy green arcade!

Then the willow-walk had not,
Haunt of love, become a spot
Fondly sought, and ne'er forgot!

Thus the graceful tree I found,
Like Estella, should be crowned
Queen of all the forest round!

Emblem—is it not?—of worth,
Beauty, truth, and gentle birth,
Bowed by sorrow down to earth.

Yes:—and still with power serene,
Modest, melancholy mien,
Live forever, lovely Queen!

Ever dear to me thou art,
Linked with being's brightest part,
Like *her* image in my heart.

Sacred Willow, still to thee
Shall my tuneful tribute be:
Fair thou art, exceedingly!

The Wind-Harp.

*   *   *   *   *   *

—THE midnight lamp was burning faintly,
Suspended from a lofty ceiling,
Within a Gothic chamber.   Sweetly
A sighing breeze, that lately roved
The moonlit lake, and graceful garden,
Yet, lover-like, no pleasure found,
No rest, though all was peace and joy,
At last the open casement entered,
Where long its serenading music
Before had sounded.

                Maiden beauty
Not here, in timid trust, awaits.

But hark, the Wind-Harp's welcoming
Comes forth to meet it!—low, at first,
And like an echo heard at eve
Among the solemn hills afar,
Or like the voice to Fancy known,
When all her soul is poesie!
Then slowly upward rolls the strain,
As if inspired by grander thoughts,
And on, still on; and silent now;
And now again a distant note
Of love and sorrow, hope and fear;
And then a tone of anger, loud

But brief, and dying off to pity!
With many a rise and many a fall,
More sweet than mortal touch may give,
The trembling strings are eloquent!

The Lovers.

THE summer moon serenely moves
   Along the deep blue sky,
And the stars look forth, and the breeze awakes,
   And glideth gently by.

And there's no sound upon the hill,
   And none adown the dale,
Save the low-toned music of a stream,
   That tells a pleasant tale:

A tale so full of melody
   That the night-birds pause to hear,
And even the sorrowful willows dance
   To the voice of the waters clear!

The summer moon glides on apace:
   Two youthful forms are seen;
And they wander hand in hand along,
   With a seeming pensive mien.

And now a song of early days—
    And now the song's no more;
And their lips have met, with a thrilling kiss—
    And——will it ne'er be o'er?

A blush—a sudden flow of tears,
    But not the tears of sorrow;
A whispered word, and a fond reply—
    And a bride will smile to-morrow!

The Court Crier.

ALEXANDER was Great, and Napoleon bold,
    Cæsar was terrible, Pompey too,
But never did mortal eye behold
    One terrible, bold and great as you:
            " Silence ! Silence !"

When the spectacled Judges take their seat,
    You solemnly march to take your own;
The clock strikes ten, you start to your feet,
    And " open the court" with trumpet tone :
            " O yes ! O yes !"

At the sound of your mighty words of law,
    The truant school-boy pants with dread,

While the negro rolls his eyes in awe,
  And shows to the Court his woolly head :
      " Hats off ! Hats off !"

Then you look majestic round and round,
  And if any there be who speaks aloud,
From your lofty chair you lightly bound,
  And force your way through the wondering crowd :
      " Come, sir ! Come, sir !"

While the Court proceeds with its grave debate,
  You practise your speeches o'er and o'er,
Till, the brain oppressed with legal weight,
  A dream curtails the solemn store :
      " Walk light ! Walk light !"

Sleep on, O Crier, most dreadful still,
  Even your slumbers startle the hall,
And your resolute snore proclaims your will,
  Seeming, instead of a tongue, to bawl :
      " Silence ! Silence !"

Flowers.

ERE Heaven's last angel flew from Eden's bowers
He sought the drooping Eve, and, offering flowers,
" Take these," he said ; " in their immortal bloom
Resides a charm to cheer thy future gloom."
16

She pressed them to her bosom, and the while
Looked up and caught the angel's holy smile.

Those flowers had been her favorites many a day,
When the glad angels thronged around her way;
O, doubly dear they were, now all was o'er,
And Eden closed, a home for her no more!

She called their music-names, and kissed them still.
The name of one, that by a happy rill
Stood modestly, she "Virtue" called, and this,
For memory's sake, received her lingering kiss—
The lily, thus since known; and, next, the rose,
Worthy to bear the name its guardian chose;
That name, save Virtue, every name above,
The soul-enchanting, Heaven-revealing "Love."

Dear were these flowers to Eve where'er she went,
Restoring Eden even in banishment,
Or whispering of an Eden yet to be,
Happy, eternal, from the Tempter free.

Dear were these flowers to Eve; and, as she died,
Calling her favorite daughters to her side,
"Take these," she said, and, in a little while
Left them the memory of an angel smile.

Since then, Eve's favorite daughters ever wear
The blooming rose, and lily, tender fair,
Are still with Virtue crowned, adorned with Love,
And that angelic smile that lures the soul above!

Gone.

Gone!   The kind, the beautiful!
    In her early bloom!
Over joyous hearts hath fallen,
    Suddenly, a gloom!

Gone!   The smile, the music tone—
    Fond, and sweet, and dear!
They were such as poets dream of:
    Seldom such appear!

Yes; beyond their brightest dreaming,
    Far surpassing all,
Shone the glory of her presence
    In her father's hall.

Life may have a thousand graces,
    By the crowd unseen;
Humble deeds of love and duty,
    Lofty, yet serene—

These were hers; and how endearing
    Those who feel may say.
No! such feelings are too sacred
    For the common day!

Round the heart, like doves, they nestle,
　　Soothing it to rest;
Till the soul looks up, triumphant,
　　Where the lost is blest!

Dead she is not, but departed
　　To the happy shore:
'T is an angel's influence pleading—
　　Weep ye, then, no more!

The Song of the Stars.

"E Pluribus Unum!"　The world with delight
Looks up to the starry blue banner of night,
In its many-blent glory rejoicing to see
AMERICA's motto, the pride of the Free!

"E Pluribus Unum!"　Our standard forever!
Woe, woe to the heart that would dare to dissever!
Shine, Liberty's stars! your dominion increase!
A guide in the battle, a blessing in peace!

"E Pluribus Unum!" And thus be, at last,
From Land unto Land our broad banner cast,
Till its Stars, like the stars of the sky, be unfurled,
In beauty and glory, embracing the world!

Woman's Faith.

AND both were pale and dying,
  On the humble cottage bed,
But still their young affection
  All its golden glory shed,
As eye to eye was speaking,
  With a calm and tender ray,
And hope immortal rising,
  Smiled the gloom of death away!

'T was beautiful to see them,
  Though a sadness, too, was there,
For Heaven's divinest graces
  Were around the wedded pair;
Yes, Love, the ever-constant,
  And the grave-triumphant Love,
With Truth, the bright reflection
  Of our GOD, who shines above!

Their lips moved slow and painful,
  And a few fond words they spoke,
But still their whispered music
  Scarce the sacred silence broke;
When came the laugh of childhood,
  And in wild and careless glee,
A boy, with cheek of roses,
  And a girl, with tresses free!

16*

The father looked upon them,
    And his eyes were dim with tears :
Alas, the grief and danger
    Of their future lonely years !
He strove with bitter anguish,
    And in sighing accents said :
' O, who will guard my children
    When I sleep among the dead !'

' Their GOD !' the mother answered,
    ' And I bless HIS holy name,
For the promise that our lone-ones
    May in HIM a father claim !
The ' ORPHAN'S GOD !' Remember !
    O, remember !'—And she died.
A smile in beauty lingered
    On the cold face by her side !

Yes, Man may soar majestic
    In the brilliant sky of mind,
But sorrow clouds his triumph,
    And he sinks, obscure and blind ;
While Woman, last from Heaven,
    Is the first to find the way,
And cheer the soul, and crown it
    With the joy of perfect day !

Anthem.

Sung in the Lodge of Sorrow, held at Washington in Memory of Ill. Bro. John Anthony Quitman, 33d, on the 30th of March, 1860, by the Supreme Council for the Southern Jurisdiction of the United States.

Weep no more!   He is not dead!
On the earth he rests his head,
But his Spirit everywhere,
Like the Sunlight, fills the air!

Weep no more!   His deeds remain,
Done on many a crimson plain,
Haunting still our flag, and told
To every breeze by every fold.

Hail to him whose burning word
Wintry Senates, kindling, heard,
While, by acclamations fanned,
Ran the fire throughout the land!

Hail to him, above the rest,
Ye who knew and loved him best,
Brethren, hail his battle done,
Earth and Heaven together won!

The Press.

Read at the Forty-second Anniversary of the Columbia Typographical Society, January 17, 1857, by THOMAS C. CONNOLLY, Esq.

DARKNESS enshrouded earth;
 And yet the sun poured undiminished light,
 And myriad stars illumed the dome of night,
  And the oft-coming moon
Renewed the lovely wonder of her birth,
  And still was fairer, till her beauty's noon
 Became angelic :—yet the earth was dark,
Or, only at far intervals, a spark,
Feeble and tremulous, responsive shone
  To all Heaven's glory !

  Alas, the sad, sad story,
The wrong, the misery, to darkness known !
 Unrecognized as brother,
  With hatred man met man;
 And Superstition cried : " Destroy each other !"
  And led the murderous van !

What if the sun shine from his proudest height ?
What if the moon and stars make fair the night ?—
  If the great world of Mind
  In darkness be confined—
There is no light !

Break through the ancient walls !
Regard no menace—Lo ! the Tyrant falls
     Dead, if defied !
Rush, resolutely on !   In yonder cell
  Knowledge is bound in chains !
Let her be free !   Let her go forth and tell
  Glad tidings ! Knowledge is the Heaven-sent bride
    The World is longing for ; and her increase
    Shall be Religion, Freedom, Love, and Peace !

Darkness retires ;
From hill to hill leap the electric fires :—
    Where yet a shade remains,
Unweariedly the Press, with giant might,
    Ever, forever,
Darts inexhaustible, all-glorious light,
    Forever !

"Pretty Polly."

MISS POLLY MARSHALL, OF THE AMERICAN THEATRE.

WHETHER tragic she, or jolly,
Where's the like of " Pretty Polly ?"

Music rises—see ! she dances !
Sunlight in her sportive glances,
On she comes, as comes the roseal
Evening cloud, when winds ambrosial

Waft it to the golden portal;
Yet, though " Pretty Polly's" mortal,
Such a glory beams around her,
That if, suddenly, we found her
Fading in her beauty's splendor,
'Mid the graces that attend her,
So to us 't would seem a vision
Should—to glory more elysian !

Gently, sweetly, ceases dancing.
Now she sings.   Her voice entrancing
Leaps at once to each affection,
Conquering all to her direction !

Then another change—and sadness
Clouds her young life's dawning gladness—
Sighs, and tears—and accents broken—
Yet her sorrow still is spoken
Music-toned ; and when, returning,
Joy is queen—her dark eyes, burning,
Cast their fairy lights, that quiver,
As the sunbeams on a river,
O'er her cheeks, her lips—illuming
All her beauty newly blooming—
And her voice flows softer, clearer,
Ever fonder, ever dearer—
Ah ! there's such a charm about her,
All's sweet with her, nought without her !

Whether tragic she, or jolly,
Where's the like of " Pretty Polly?"

A Dry-Goods Store.

HE stood behind the counter,
　And a smile was on his face;
And a maiden was before him,
　In that ceiling-lighted place;
And calico, ten pieces,
　Unrolled between them lay:
And thus the clerk and customer
　Were wearing out the day!

He told her this would wash,
　And he told her that was fine,
And he called her close attention
　To the beautiful design;
And a Secretary's lady
　Bought twenty yards of this—
" And shall I cut you off the same?
　I know you 'll like it, Miss!"

No, no, she could n't—would n't—
　But she thought she 'd rather look
At a piece of purple silk—and yet
　No piece of silk she took!
Then gloves—they were " too large;"
　Then ribbons—" all too plain :"—
And the pile grew higher, higher;
　And she said—she 'd " call again!"

Alas, alas, poor clerk !
  My heart was full of sorrow
At all thy fruitless labor—
  The same, perchance, to-morrow !—
To stand, and talk, and smile,
  And spread thy goods about ;
Yet find thy stratagems too weak
  To lure a sixpence out !

Thou surely must be something
  Or more or less than man,
For looking still as pleasantly
  As ere the siege began ;
Replacing all the pieces,
  And smoothing them to rest,
Even as a loving mother
  Calms her babe upon her breast !

Job is not dead : he liveth
  Most patiently in thee,
His wondrous gentleness improved,
  As all the world may see !
Thou lookest like an angel,
  And surely art no less !—
Such height of admiration
  No language may express !

𝔓𝔦𝔩𝔤𝔯𝔦𝔪𝔰.

LITTLE we know,
And in our ignorance too oft rebel.
  GOD looks in pity on our darkling woe:
" HE doeth all things well!"

" Knowledge is power:"
Knowledge is Virtue, were a nobler truth;
  Heaven's light, and crown, and beatific dower;
The soul's eternal youth!

Abroad through time,
Lost children, cheated by our hopes and fears,
  We wander, and recall some home-taught rhyme,
The music of the spheres!

And thus, amid
The discords, which are passions of the Earth—
  Like birds within a sombre forest hid,
Sing joys of holier birth!

Our lives resemble
The mystic breathings of the wild wind's lute—
  Mournful forever—and the accents tremble—
Are sweetest sad—then mute.

Hosanna!

"Like ships at sea, while in above the world."
Night Thoughts.

PROUDLY o'er the conquered ocean,
  All her sails in sunlight flashing,
  Back her prow the white foam dashing,
Like a warrior, home returning,
  Bounds the eager bark !
O, she dared an awful battle,
Lightning wrath, and thunder rattle,
  Billows dread and dark !

Even when the deep was smiling,
  When the rainbow bent above her,
  When the breeze, a minstrel lover,
Songs of beauty softly singing,
  Sought her placid breast;
When the nautilus came gladly—
Still the bark remembered sadly,
  'T was a syren's rest !

Only to destruction luring,
  Trust her not, she never sleepeth,
  Cruel watch and ward she keepeth,
For the weak, unwary stranger,
  O'er the lost below.

Bravely on, with constant pinion!
See! beyond her false dominion,
  Friendly Islands glow!

Soul immortal, Heaven-descended!
  Destined for the Isles of Beauty!
  'T is thy GOD-directed duty,
With the World's wild ocean warring,
  With its fatal peace,
Thitherward to point thy banner,
Bearing brilliantly: "HOSANNA!"
  Till thy warfare cease.

Fear thou not, whatever peril,
  Dark, deceitful, may assail thee;
  Never shall thy Compass fail thee:
Never, though thy way seem lonely,
  Shalt thou be alone:
Oft a mystic Light appearing,
Oft a Music, soft and cheering,
  Strange, prophetic tone!

Light and music, gloom and discord,
  Long upon the deep beguiling,
  Mingle with eternal smiling
Now around the Isles of Beauty,
  Round the happy shore:
Angel forms of love are meeting:
Hark their ecstasy of greeting:
  'Rest! and roam no more!'

Love's Adventure.

In a day of cold December,
  Love was flying round ;
Seeing on my hearth an ember :
  "Ha !" said he, "'t is found !"
With his wings he fanned the fire,
  Till a blaze it grew,
Warmer, brighter, higher, higher :
  "This," said he, " will do !"

But, alack for Love, unthinking,
  'Mid his glad employ !
Out a flame leaps, while he 's winking,
  Burns his wings, poor boy !
" Now," said weeping Love, " all 's over !
  Who can count the cost !
Just about to ' live in clover '—
  Annie Hilton 's lost !"

" *Annie Hilton !* What ! you know her !"
  Breathless I exclaimed.
" That do I !" said Love, " and owe her
  All for which I 'm famed !
How to wreathe my lips, she taught me !
  How to move my eyes !
O, the bliss her lessons brought me !"—
  Then the rest was sighs.

Touched with pity: "Dear one, hither!
    Come to me:" I said,
"Where I keep her image"—Whither,
    Think you, had he fled?
Why, I heard him laugh, that minute:
    "Here I am!—your heart!
Don't be scared—I'm snugly in it,
    And I won't depart!

"No, I won't depart, though lonely,
    Somewhat, is the place;
You must take me where—where only—
    Smiles an angel face—
Annie Hilton's! But, before it,
    Find an Album bright,
Choose a rosy page, and o'er it
    Love's adventure write!

"Send the book to gentle Annie,
    With a word or two;
Seal the note, lest Mary, Fannie,
    Jane, should talk of you!
So shall Annie Hilton know it—
    That she is most dear:—
I will add a postscript, Poet!
    Yes, and date it *here!*"

Mary Ellen.

I have but pleasant thoughts of thee,
   I cannot weep, though thou art dead ;
To weep would seem impiety,
   A wrong unto thy spirit fled :
For in thy life such beauty shone,
I can have pleasant thoughts alone !

I look upon thy placid face—
   Thine eyes illume it not—'tis cold ;
Thy pale, still lips—no more I trace
   Their smile. But unimpaired I hold
A living impress in my heart,
And love it. It can not depart !

I gaze upon thee. No! 'tis thou
   Who lookest from thy home above,
Thyself a viewless angel now,
   Rejoicing in OUR FATHER'S love :—
And *this*—the image of my friend,
To mark her journey's happy end !

Yes, in the bright Eternal Land,
   Beyond the tearful Vale of Tombs,
First welcomed by thy Sister's hand,
   Thou rovest. And the sweet rose blooms,
Without a thorn. The waters flow
In music. White wings come and go !

Thou canst not visit us again,
　　Nor would I that thou shouldst return;
Thy lot is bliss, our own is pain—
　　But thus the gold of love we earn,
And win the prize.　Thou hast it!　Well
Thy pilgrimage the way doth tell!

Two Fables from the Polish.

ANTHONY GOREÇKI.

I.

THE CORONATION.

A Greenfinch said to a Swallow: "Whither
　　This crowd of magpies, ravens, crows?"
"To-day there will be a Coronation;
And each one hurries to his station—
　　Good reason, everybody knows!
For *meet* reward allures them thither!"
　　　　"But who the King?"
　　　　"Ah, that's the thing!
A shrewd one! To decide the claim
In true legitimacy's name,
And universal peace to keep,
The Wolf himself will be King o' the Sheep!"

II.

The Cat and the Mouse.

A Mouse was eating a book.   A Cat,
  Quietly passing by,
Said to the Mouse: "Now why is that?"
  "Because," was the Mouse-reply,
  "The book contains a lie—
Yes, an impudent lie of *you!*"
" Whether the book be false or true,
Know, Sir Mouse, the Press is free,
And I am King, and it so shall be!"
Then, for example's sake, he took
For dinner the Mouse that dined on the book!

When you are a Mouse in the paws of a Cat,
Justice is sure!   Rely on that!

Man and Woman.

WHEN Man was lost in Paradise,
  It was a grievous thing, no doubt;
But, by her own fair sacrifice,
  A Woman—bless her!—helped him out!

Hymen.

HYMEN was a Grecian youth,
    Dwelling by the sea.
Gold he had not : love and truth
    Were his treasurie—
Wealth that is no care to keep,
Crown of joy and balm of sleep !

Happy as the breeze that bore
Music to the blooming shore ;
Happy as the liberal waves,
Showering diamonds in the caves ;
Blessed as heaven's blue arch above,
Lit with truth, and breathing love.

O'er so beautiful a life
    Must there come a cloud ?
Nature with herself at strife !
    Fair—and yet so proud !
Maiden of the palace, see !
Hymen's love were grace for thee !

Bending servitors of state—
What if love himself should wait ?
Hollow words of purchased praise—
Love's one whisper bliss conveys !
Gemmed tiara, glittering chains—
Love's light hand more wealth contains !

No : she scorns the lover's vow.
    Maiden, still beware !
Even Olympus' height will bow
    To a lover's prayer !
Love will conquer Earth, and rise,
Conqueror yet, to rule the skies !

'Twas a gay-robed page, who sought
Service, and all favor brought,
Such as gentle wiles reveal,
Such as youth and beauty seal ;
So the lady's will he gained,
So the service sought obtained.

Evening's placid hour : the sun
    Hallowing the scene.
Wanders forth the lovely one,
    'Mid her gardens green—
Wanders by the lonely shore—
Pondering, looks the waters o'er.

Still companion of her walk,
Silent all his pleasing talk,
Pondering too—but other ways,
Faithful page, thy fancy strays :—
Not the garden—not the sky—
Not the great sea slumbering nigh.

Suddenly from out the trees
    Darts a robber band—
Swiftly bears them o'er the seas,
    Far from native land !

Little now remains of joy:
" Hope !" implores the smiling boy.

Hope ! it was the spirit bright,
Heart-guest, in Despair's despite ;
Hope ! that, as each morrow came,
Fondly whispered one sweet name;
Hope ! that by the stars and moon
Whispered still : ' I come—and soon !'

Long to tell, nor need be told,
    How the gentle page
'Mid the savage band grew bold,
    Saving from their rage—
Terrible far more, their lust—
Her who had no other trust.

Long the story were to tell,
How, when night and tempest fell,
Safely from the wine-drugged band
Went the captives, hand in hand,
Hand in hand, with bending form,
Lighted by the fitful storm !

Then upon the sea—and lo !
    Native land in sight,
Gorgeous in the golden glow
    Of the sunset light !
Soft upon the tinted blue
Rose the pillared walls to view !

' Home again ! Ah, but for thee,
  Home no more had been for me !

What reward'——
                    Thy love!
                              ' 'T is thine!'
Thou art love!   To-day, be mine!
Hymen waits thy answer!—' Yes;'
Tears, embrace, and kiss confess!

Lovers' hope and dream of life,
      Every loving vow,
Imaged Hymen—Hymen's wife—
      Love's ideal now!
Smiles and honors crowned their praise,
Happiness their halcyon days!

Temples to another god,
On the hills where Hymen trod—
On the hills of distant lands!—
Lovers, come! and, taking hands,
Give your heart-vow to his name:
Joy to Hymen! love and fame!

Oliver Cromwell.

[FROM AN UNFINISHED TRAGEDY.]

ACT I. SCENE 2. Night. Library in the cottage of Milton. A casement open. The music of an organ is heard, from an inner apartment. ELIZABETH discovered, listening. Music ceases. Enter MILTON.

Eliz. The daintiest music that I ever heard!
Why is it, father, that 't is new to me?
Mil. Because it came to-night from yon fair Moon!
Eliz. Only composed to-night! -
Mil.   A prelude, daughter;
I trust a prelude to a happy strain,
Which even now is murmuring at my heart.
As yet, the hour is early: ere I sleep,
I 'll write some rhyming words—two songs, mayhap;
And "L' Allegro" shall be the name of one;
And of its shadow—what? "Il Penseroso."
Eliz. Stories of Italy?
Mil.   But seeming so:
The scene shall be in England.——
And part of it is round our own dear porch.
Eliz. The vines, the little garden?
Mil.   Yes, of those
A loving word or two: the porch may be
The frame-work of the picture. Something thus:

"Through the sweet-brier, or the vine,
Or the twisted eglantine"——

Eliz. I know it will be beautiful! Your touch
Can make our simple garden, Paradise!

Mil. (*Aside.*) The garden—Paradise!——-
There is a thought in that; it pleases me:
Paradise Lost—a mournful, wondrous theme!
Yes, I will ponder it.

Eliz.   What think you, father?

Mil. Only of trifles, in the eyes of men.
The age is stormed with troubles! presently
Shall peace return; and then my lofty song,
My universal song, shall win the world,
Who will not let it die!

Eliz.   His mind is crowded
With its mysterious guests. I ever know
When fancies press upon him. So, good night!
His magic wants no witnesses. Dear father,
I go to do my copying: the task
Is nearly finished.

Mil. (*Abstractedly.*)   Would to Heaven 'twere done!

Eliz. I do my best—

Mil.   Right patiently and well.
But not of that I spoke: not words, my daughter;
The swiftly-coming future teems with deeds,
And those, I fear, of blood! O, Liberty!
Is there no music welcome unto thee
But sighs and groans and shrieks! No offering
But human hearts, piled, quivering, on thy altar!
Must thou behold the widow's agony;
The orphan's helplessness; the death of pity;
Ere thou wilt smile to bless us!

Eliz.   Speak not thus!
Surely it is a dream! England is safe!

These sorrows are thin clouds; the light shines through,
And brighter still; to chase them far away!
   Mil. It may be, but mine eyes shall never see it!
   Eliz. Why not? Have patience yet a little while.
   Mil. I shall not see it!
   Eliz.   Why, dear father, why?
   Mil. Dost thou forget?
   Eliz.   Forget?—
   Mil.   There comes a darkness
Over my eyes, at times, that, as I write,
Changes the paper to a sombre gray,
In which the words do fade, like stars at morning!
   Eliz. My poor, dear father, wilt thou not, for me,
For one who loves thee—yea! with all her soul—
Wilt thou not rest? Wilt not refrain these studies,
That so devour thy sight?
   Mil. There's one who urges me to constant toil,
One whom I love even better than my daughter—
England! For her sake, grant me power, O Heaven,
To labor on! Like Sampson, blind yet strong,
Let me defy the enemies of freedom,
Hug the huge pillars of the tyrant's temple,
And crush it to the earth—though I, too, perish!
Not for a day, not for a day, O GOD!
I work for centuries; and grope in darkness
That light may shine for millions yet to be!
   Eliz. The deed is grand. I almost worship that,
But still I love my father, and would save him.
   Mil. Be brave, my child; for kind thou ever wert,
Obedient ever. Thy reward is sure.
Remember, then, I, too, obey *my* FATHER!
Now to thy chamber; write no more to-night:

And I will only whisper to the Moon,
An hour at most, then hie me to repose.
Good night!
    Eliz.   Good night!
    Mil.   And in thy prayer—
    Eliz.   As ever! [*Exit.*]

MILTON crosses to the casement, and gazes upward.

Mil. Beautiful light!   Beautiful lamp of Heaven!
What marvel that the heathen worshipped thee?
That from a thousand hills their altars sent
The silvery smoke of adoration up?
Not knowing HIM, the ONE, the UNCREATE,
What marvel thou shouldst seem a DEITY,
The first-born offspring of HIS earliest gift,
And blesséd emanation from HIS glory!—
For I, HIS favored servant, strive in vain
To wean my heart from thee!   Though, soon, no more
Shall I behold thy spirit-soothing smile.
A dread and everlasting midnight comes.
What duty, then, remains?   Why, still to labor,
That mental blindness follow not!

Enter ANDREW.

And. There be a man on the porch.
Mil. Robber, or honest man?
And. Verily, he should be honest, for he looketh not
like a Cavalier; and his name is Cromwell.
Mil. Why came he not in?
And. In good sooth, and of a verity, because I did not
ask him; but rather did desire he should wait without,

till it should be plain unto me that you reclined not, even in the arms of Somebody.

Mil. Somnus were moré correct.

And. We live and learn; yea, and verily do we learn more evil than good. For the times are full of wickedness, yea, and of abomination; and the bishops persecute the people, and the King, like unto another Cæsar, would grind the Parliament under his iron heel, but for such a friend of liberty, such a noble soldier of the LORD, as brave Master Cromwell——

Mil. Who waits in the chilly night!

And. I will go straightway, and admit that faithful servant——

Mil. As thou art one thyself.

And.   Yea, verily!   [*Exit.*]

Mil. His words are wrong, but those are from the lips. His life is right, and that is from the heart.

Enter CROMWELL.

Give you good evening, Cromwell.

Crom.   Master Milton,
The LORD be over you!

Mil. I cry you pardon that you stood without.

Crom. Nay, but a moment, with the pleasant moon—
The only pleasant thing in England's night!
Nor, were there blame, were you the least to blame—
And Andrew did his duty civilly.
Ne'erless, there is a fault: and I cry pardon,
Intruding on your studies.

Mil.   Of a truth,
Good Cromwell, you are ever welcome here.

Crom. I thought so, and I came :—especially—

Mil. With news?

18*

*   *   *   *   *   *   *
*   *   *   *   *   *   *
*   *   *   *   *   *   *

Mil. But of the King?

Crom.   Ay, of the King!   Well said!
Have I not told you horrors?

Mil.   Too, too many;
Save that, at last, they may arouse our England!

Crom. They shall! From Parliament I'll thunder them,
Round all the sea-girt coast! But what—what think you?
What name for him who leads this mad rebellion?
'Tis England's King!

Mil. The King?   Can this be proved?

Crom.   It can : and is!

Mil. Then is there cause to fear! No life is safe!
Woe to the man who dares uplift his voice
For England's Constitution and her Church!
But now we see our enemy.   Forewarned,
'Tis our own fault if not foreweaponed, too!

Crom. I watch for that !———
With girded loins, and burning lamps, I watch!
And to this end now do I come to you.
What of the youth, Ardenne?

Mil.   Right well of him.
I kept my messenger on guard, who found him,
To-day, the very hour of his arrival;
Gave him the letters—

Crom.   Answered he at all?

Mil. Read the reply.   (*Giving Cromwell a letter.*)
Crom. (*Reading; and speaking aloud at times.*)
                    We wrestled with the LORD;
Yea, with the LORD in prayer.   I tell you truth,

I do profess; it came unto our minds
As with an audible and potent voice :
' Call to your aid the man—even the youth—
Edgar Ardenne !'   He answers :   " Here am I !"
Mil. 'Twas well our offer had no bribery in't,
Nor aught of doubt, nor word of one condition !
This do I know : he is a worshipper
Of wisdom, truth, and liberty !   To these,
Let him once see the way, he will not fail,
Though at the price of all he holds most dear,
To follow it !
 Crom.   Why came he not to-day ?
 Mil.   I know not.   Still
There is good reason.   He will surely come.
 Crom. I do begin to doubt him.   Let him not,
In promises, take Charles for an example—
His Majesty, the Liar !
 Mil.   Be assured.

Enter ARDENNE.

 Ard. Milton !
 Mil. Ardenne !   Most welcome home !   My friend,
Oliver Cromwell.
 Ard. (*Aside.*)   Mabel's prophecy !
(*To Cromwell.*) Sir, I rejoice to meet you. I have heard,
Even in a single day, my first in England,
The story of your life.
 Crom.   A simple story,
Nor worth the telling.   In the hands of HIM,
Whom I would serve, I am a blade of grass,
But if it be HIS will to give me strength,

Yea, as the warrior's spear I may be strong,
To do His Holy bidding.
    Mil. (*To Ard.*)   Troublous times
Have darkened England, since I saw you last.
That moonlight night, more beautiful than ours,
Musing within the haunted Coliseum,
Our pensiveness was for the glorious past,
The old renown of Rome—not England's fall.
    Crom.   The fall of England!
Truly it will be so, unless her children
Rise to the rescue! England's fall—the World's!
Religion, Freedom, have no home but here:
If here they dwell not, they return to Heaven,
And leave the race of man in deeper doom.
    Ard. The news to-day—it went in whispers by me—
Can it be true—the King?
    Mil.   It is too true!
    Crom. A damnéd crime! Too black to think upon!
A thousand hearts this day will blaze in England,
At telling of the wrong! A thousand arms
Be ready to avenge it! Insult, first,
Then persecution, tyranny, and murder!
We have no laws, but by his high permission;
We have no liberty, save he may grant it;
We have no faith, but his, the LORD's Anointed!
We have—no English blood!
    Ard. (*Aside.*)   O, woe to me,
That such things are: and Mabel, woe to thee;
Thou, in thy love, to deem thy love a traitor,
To scorn his love, because he loves his honor!
And thou, old man, my poor heart-broken father,
Deceived in all thy hopes, down to the grave

Tottering with rapid steps, and leaving me
Thy heritage, a curse!

Mil.   Ardenne!

Ard.   I listen.

Mil. Too much unto thyself: To England more!
Cromwell!

Crom.   Pardon me;
My thoughts were down at Huntingdon.

Mil.   Recall them.

Crom. I try: they circle England!   Nowhere rest!

Mil. Band them with all the best of English thoughts,
And so consult—decide!   To Liberty
Be thou our Leader!

Crom.   I, an humble man,
The weakest of the servants of the LORD!

Ard. Let me be first to say: I follow Cromwell!

Enter the SPIRIT.

Crom. Beautiful! Terrible!   Thou comest again!
Why dost thou visit me?

Mil. (*To Ard.*)   It is a mood
That doth at times oppress him.   In his youth
Such seasons were.   But this will pass anon.

Ard. Look now!   As one that suffers agony,
He battles with the unresisting air,
Gazes on vacancy, and speaks to nothing.

Mil. Disturb him not.

Crom.   O, answer, answer me!
It will not!   See! it moves! see! see! 'tis still!
   (*Grasping Milton.*) I told you this had been, and you
      believed not!
Look for yourself!   'Tis there!   But no, no, no:

It is not for the touch!   Could I but grasp it—
I would compel reply: now I entreat!
   Spirit. Cromwell!
   Crom.   A voice! Or do I dream—
   Spirit.   Hail, Cromwell!
A deed invites thee, and thou shalt not fail!
Cromwell, *the first in England*————
   Crom. (*Eagerly.*)   Speak!
   Spirit.   All hail!   [*Exit Spirit.*]

   Characters stand grouped; as the curtain falls, mysterious and distant triumphant music.

END OF ACT I.

Note.—It was a common story among the contemporaries of Cromwell, even before his attainment of high *military* rank, that he had been awaked from his sleep, when a boy, by *a shape,* which told him he should be *the greatest man in England;* but not using the word *King.*

SONNETS TO FRIENDS.

———

> "These to the few,
> Who have been ministers of peace to me,
> Strength to my mind, and honey to my heart."

I.

Rev. Dr. John C. Smith.

WASHINGTON.

To thee, the friend of many days, I bring
These tribute words, a full heart's offering,
Less that the world may see how much I owe thee,
  More that the world may see thy merit more,
  And learn, through thee, thy FATHER to adore,
HIS laws obeying.   There are none below thee,
For thou hast made them brothers; none above,
For what too high to comprehend in love?
Thy life is like a perfumed breeze, out-going
  From some delightful, flower-adornéd land,
  With "healing on its wings," and blessings bland,
Grateful and viewless in its ever-flowing.
On Earth, what happy souls acknowledge thee!
In Heaven, what welcome shall thy presence be!

II.

Rev. Dr. G. W. Samson.

PRESIDENT OF COLUMBIAN COLLEGE, WASHINGTON.

THOU who hast grown upon our love through years,
  Whose smiles have ever added to our pleasure,
Whose gentle voice hath soothed away our tears,
  Whose thoughtful mind enriched our own minds' treasure,
And now who art, on yonder classic height,
  The guide of youth, companion, father, friend,
Banding their hearts, that they in love unite,
  And learn that wisdom is a means, not end :
To thee these words of gratitude belong,
  Part for myself, but more that thou art good,
That in the world-war GOD hath made thee strong,
  And others, from thy deeds, have understood
And done their own true duty. Thou hast trod
The Holy Land of Earth : thou shalt tread that of GOD !

III.

William Henry Donoho.

BROTHER, indeed, thou hast been in my joy,
  Brother, indeed, thou hast been in my sorrow,
Proving such sympathy, while yet a boy,
  As gave sad token for some future morrow,
Sad unto thee, perchance, but glad to others :
The poet's tears baptize the world as brothers !
So, in thy manhood, often have I known
  Many with circling praise receive thy song,
Undreaming it was built upon a moan.
  So weep the dewy stars the chill night long,
And when before the sun the dark is flown,
  The drops are diamonds ! Grief, and pain, and wrong,
Inspire the poet; and he sings, and dies.
Despair not ! Love is Queen, though crowned but in the
    skies !

IV.

James E. Murdoch.

MURDOCH, thy live rendition of the ages
  Night after night have I with profit known,
Watching how love-thought o'er the poet's pages
  Had made each treasure-bearing word thy own.
  The poet was the harp, whose native tone
Thine was the grace to give the world again:
And never didst thou seek, as many vain,
  The Actor's glory to present alone.
Thou wast content to be reflected light,
  Like yonder half-retiring western star,
  Winning the wondering looks of men afar,
Who, dazzled, could not reach the Day-God's height.
Yet, when thy transient borrowed sheen was done,
I thought not of the Star, for Murdoch was the Sun!

V.

J. Henry Dmochowski.*

SCULPTOR.

THOU, when in prison gloom for Liberty,
  Nature denied, wast visited by Art,
  Who gave such light and gladness to thy heart,
In thy soul's freedom seemed thy body free!
In after years, when Poland was no more,
Camest thou, an Exile, to our happy shore,
And woke to see all realized the dream
  Thou wouldst have realized for native land;
And freedom then was dearest, till a theme,
  Yet dearer, Love taught, and enchained thy hand
In flowery bondage.   That a day should beam
  So fair—so fleeting !   Now thy household band
Hath home in Heaven : yet also on the Earth :
Thine art, informing stone, hath eternized their worth !

* J. H. D. SAUNDERS.

19*

VI.

John Mitchel.

Lover of Erin, banished from her breast,
What clime, however fair, shall give thee rest?
And yet no maddened wanderer wilt thou go,
   Crying aloud against unpitying Fate,
For thou lovest wisely, not like Romeo,
   And with resolvéd heart wilt watch and wait.
Thy Juliet sleeps, but not the sleep of death—
And there is magic in thy true lips' breath!
They knew it well, who banished thee afar,
   And changed from isle to isle thy prison doom,
And were too weak to hold thee! Lo! the bar,
   Torn from thy dungeon—and the ponderous tomb
Shudders at every shock! Thy Juliet hears!
She lives! She shall be thine through many glorious years!

VII.

Albert Pike.

Bold in the right, and beautiful as bold,
    Stands forth thy soul before the world's proud eyes;
To Gods and Men thy golden truths are told,
    Like sunbeams piercing through the clouds' disguise,
Defiant of their storm, and still more bright
For all the foldings of their thunderous night.
Not one art thou, an April bard, to rain
    A few weak drops upon the thirsting earth,
Then with a smile, unfeeling, fickle, vain,
Come gaily forth to take thy gift again,
    And kill the flowers just struggling into birth.
No! as a tempest, gathering o'er the main,
Thou hurlest from the rock strong Error's towers;
And Truth her temple builds, 'mid amaranthine bowers!

VIII.

John Savage.

JOHN the Divisible: for thou art many,
  Yet, like our Union, one.   Where wit is found,
  No brighter word than thine goes laughing round;
Thy song, or gay or sad, is sweet as any;
Thy story moves to tears of grief or gladness;
  Thy poesie is from the heart's deep mine,
Dewy with morning, tinged with twilight sadness,
  Smiling and weeping—all the world's—and thine.
When "Waiting for a Wife" is on the stage,
  Merriment's music rings from heart to heart;
  When "Sybil," victim of a traitor's art,
From soul to soul runs the electric rage.
Thus art thou many—each entire—all one:
By many loved for each—my love excluding none!

IX.

E. Kingman.

EVER will I remember with delight
  Strawberry Knoll; not for the berries red,
  As, ere my time, the vines were out of bed,
And gone; but many a day and many a night
Have given me argument to love it well,
  Whether in Summer, 'neath its perfumed shade,
  Whether by moonlight's magic wand arrayed,
Or when in Winter's lap the rose-leaves fell.
For pleasant faces ever there were found,
  For genial welcome ever met me there,
And thou, my friend, when Thought went smiling round,
  Madest her calm look, reflecting thine, more fair.
Those who have known thee as a Statesman, know
Thy noon-day: I have felt thy great heart's sunset glow!

X.

W. W. Seaton.

FRIEND of my father, ere my life began;
My friend, from playful Youth to pensive Man;
Though now the white hairs gather on my head,
　　Though now my winter days are coming fast,
Still, with a mingled feeling, love and dread,
　　Do I approach thee, as in years far passed:
No less to-day thy kindness is than then,
And more of honors hast thou won from men.
Won worthily.　They knew, in honoring thee,
　　From the rich circlet of their gift would flow
　　Unwonted beauty, and a kindling glow,
To cheer and guide them.　Such is Heaven's decree:
Whom good men seek, from self-selected shade,
Their trust, his truth, shall many times be paid!

XI.

Clark Mills.

INAUGURATION OF HIS EQUESTRIAN STATUE OF WASHINGTON, FEBRUARY 22D, 1860.

TO-DAY I stood beside thee, when the crowd
Sent to the heavens their acclamations proud,
Echoed by cannon, and in martial strains
    Of music fading. For, in sunset's glow,
    That moment WASHINGTON appeared! I know
What strong joy leaped through all thy burning veins!
Even in my own was scarce a feebler joy,
Thy task well done, which Time can not destroy!
What need hast thou for measured words like mine?
    In two heroic forms thou speakest ever!
Let me in friendship link my name with thine,
    Thine of a chain no power of Earth can sever!
If not of fame, I have such claim of thee:
I sought to cheer thy gloom; thy gladness share with me!

XII.

Maye.

AMONG my friends, is one, most dear of all,
With many love-names. I can scarce recall
My life beyond the time when her I found;
   My life, before that happy day, was dark;
Some timid joy across my path would bound,
   As a swift deer, which, ere the eye can mark
Its form distinctly, is not! And the gloom
That filled the forest deepens like a tomb!
But she, O she has lingered at my side,
   And from her delicate and loving heart
A light, a constant light, has been my guide,
   Chasing all fearful shadows far apart.
Many the blessings GOD has given to me :
HE crowned them all, dear MAYE, in giving thee !

GOLDSMITH OF PADUA.

A Drama, in Three Acts.

20

TO

C. W. TAYLEURE, Esq.,

DIRECTOR OF THE WASHINGTON THEATRE, UNDER WHOSE AUSPICES IT WAS
FIRST ACTED,

"THE GOLDSMITH OF PADUA"

Is Dedicated,

WITH ADMIRATION FOR HIS TALENTS AS A DRAMATIC AUTHOR, AND
RESPECT FOR HIS CHARACTER AS A MAN.

PERSONS REPRESENTED.

[AS ORIGINALLY PRODUCED AT THE WASHINGTON THEATRE, NOVEMBER 8, 1858.]

Vincenti	Mr. H. F. DALY.
Guisseppe	Mr. FORRESTER.
Grumio	Mr. J. M. DAWSON.
Count Ferando	Mr. J. HARRISON.
The Judge	Mr. M. LANAGAN.
Tranio	Mr. J. M. BARRON.
Jeronimo	Mr. T. S. HOLLAND.
Beppo	Mr. J. WHITING.
Cosmo	Mr. LEWIS.
Jacobo	Mr. WARD.
Bianca	Miss J. PARKER.
Nina	Mrs. C. W. TAYLEURE.
Florio, a Page	Mrs. PROCTOR.

Lords and Ladies, Officer of the Court of Justice, Citizens, &c.

TIME: End of the Fifteenth Century.

SCENE: Padua.

20*

THE GOLDSMITH OF PADUA.

ACT I.

Jac. There be some men who talk of hearts!   In sooth,
I understand them not : but this I know—
Such men are always poor!   I 'd rather own
A thousand ducats than a thousand hearts,
With all their lofty words of truth and honor!
Their lofty words no eloquence possess
Like *these*—which move all hearts, and heads, and hands!
     (*Showing a purse of gold.*)
Seignior Vincenti
Is *thus* the greatest orator of Padua!
But who comes yonder?   Gazing up and down,
Like some poor fellow from the untaught fields,
First visiting the city!   How he stares!

Enter Tranio.

Tra. Wonderful! splendid!
Jac.   Ha! I know the lad :
Wild as the woods he left!
Tra.   A glorious palace!

Jac. Tranio!

Tra.　　Who calls?

Jac.　　　　Do you not see?

Tra. Why—yes—Jacobo? Is it so, indeed?
I thought you many a league away!

Jac.　　　　No doubt:
And just as well I might have been, good Tranio,
For all the use your eyes were!

Tra.　　　　Pardon me.
I only came to Padua to-day;
And yonder palace did, in truth, surprise me.
Who dwells there?

Jac. Seignior Vincenti.

Tra.　　　　What a noble Prince!

Jac. Only a Goldsmith.

Tra.　　　　Ha!

Jac.　　　　A wealthy one,
Surpassing princes; and, if they be German——

Tra. (*Imitating him.*) "If they be German"——

Jac. Quite rich enough to make a score of them!
Daily come travelers, with coin to change,
Piling his coffers till they overflow!
Few die, relationless, but he's executor.
Many pay tribute to his wealth and fame,
By leaving him their heir. The city gives him
All public contracts. He is almost sunk
Beneath the weight of trusts and offices,
Not merely offered, but imposed upon him!

Tra. Now, by Saint Paul! the happiest man alive!
Can such things be?

Jac.　　　　All true. My lord, Guisseppe,

A merchant here, hath many dealings with him.
Guisseppe's clerk should, therefore, know the Goldsmith.
   Tra. A clerk !
How is it, if I ask your aid, Jacobo?
My lot is such I'd willingly exchange it,
And hardly fear a worse one.
   Jac. I know a place that will precisely suit :
And I've no wit or you've the place to-day.
   Tra.   Thanks, thanks, my friend !
   Jac. We'll talk more privately of these affairs.

                             [*Exeunt.*]

Scene II.—*Garden of Vincenti's Palace. Enter* Ferando *and* Bianca, *followed by* Nina, *who is gathering flowers.*

   Fer. (*Aside.*)   I *would* speak, and I *cannot.*   Strange,
      that Love,
In his first coming but a feeble boy,
Yet when he lays his finger on the heart—
O such a weight is there, it scarce can move,
And the late voluble, imperious lips,
Like timid slaves, do closely cling together,
Silent and motionless.
   Bian. (*Smiling.*)   A pleasant evening.
   Fer. Yes—terrible, Bianca :—that is—pleasant.
   Bian. Why, what's the matter?
   Fer.   Nothing.   Did I speak ?
   Bian. Surely; and still said—nothing. 'Tis the fashion;
But as so much of it is offered me,
I weary of it; Yesterday, to-day,
To-morrow, and for many a day to come,
Has been, and is, and will be, nothing—nothing.
Nothing has many ways of saying nothing :

Last night, he told me, at Guisseppe's villa,
That Homer, could he visit earth once more,
Indeed would paint a Venus!   That was nothing.
And at another time he said my robe
Was like a silvery cloud, and I the moon,
That gave it radiance!   That again was nothing.
And nothing talks of blushes, lips, and eyes,
And sometimes writes me sonnets, sings me songs,
Taking much trouble—also taking cold—
To tell the deaf night, 'neath my balcony,
That nothing has a heart!

  Fer.   So fair and cruel!

  Bian. Well done, Sir Count!   A good exordium:
On with the speech!   'T is the true tone of nothing!

  Fer. Thou art too light, Bianca.   'Neath the leaf,
The frail and fluttering leaf, the rich fruit lies:
The royal heart beneath a poor disguise.

  Bian. Nay, if thou bringest rhyme, I fly at once.
'T is the bad spirit hath tormented me;
I cannot bear his buzzing.   (*Going.*)

  Fer.   Stay and listen.

  Bian. To loves and doves, and hearts and darts?

  Fer. (*Impressively.*)   Bianca!
Listen to truth, of which these rhymes are symbols,
Often ill-used, by vanity and folly;
But, dear Bianca——

  Bian. (*Aside.*) " *Dear* Bianca!"

  Nina. (*Listening, aside.*)   " Dear!"

  Fer. I have to-day few words of any kind,
And even many, of the best, were useless:
I can but say: I love thee!

  Nina.   " Love!"   I knew it!
O Grumio! Grumio! only say "I love thee!"

Fer. Dearest girl!
I am not one to swear by all the saints,
And Cupid chief, how wondrously I love thee;
To sigh, to weep, to fall upon my knees,
As to a goddess: no! I am a man,
Feeling man's native dignity—and thou
Art but a woman—a true, noble woman—
Worthy a man's best love.   Nature and fortune
Both have done much for thee.   Thy beauty, sweet,
Would win the worldling: though I prize it, too,
'T is as a picture of the angel soul:
And, for the splendor of thy life's estate,
The golden frame that bounds the charming picture,
I own it is not valueless, but still
Only thyself I love; and here, in proof,
All that is good, faithful, and fond in me,
I dedicate to thy superior merit,
Now and forever!
    Bian.   Dost thou love me, then?
    Fer. Dost doubt me?
    Bian.   Doubt?   I only doubt myself,
As worthy of such love :—for such I prize,
Beyond all beauty, all the world can give,
As Heaven's divinest boon!
    Fer.   To Heaven the praise!
So shall our lives go smiling through the vale,
Cheering its shadows with a sacred light,
And hand in hand climb the Eternal Height!
                        (Music within.)
What means this music?
    Bian.   'T is a preparation—
A certain festival—an anniversary——

Fer. Thine own—thy birth-night.

Bian.   Marvelous memory!

Fer. No marvel, love, that Memory should pale
Before the light of Hope!—
                              I will attend thee,
But here [*his heart*] is such a festival, Bianca,
With angel guests, with whisperings, with music,
All so ecstatic, that I fear me still
I shall forget myself, and wandering go,
Like a poor ghost, through good Vincenti's halls.

   Bian. Poor ghost: *I* shall be there!

   Fer.   And *here!* [*his heart.*]
Two festivals at once :—
But this the better and the dearer one!
Then, for awhile, farewell!   Our contract, sweet,
                              (*Enter* JERONIMO, *back.*)
Is yet deficient——

   Bian.   Wanting what?

   Fer. (*Kisses her.*)   'T is perfect!

   Jer. A kiss!   (*Aside.*)   (*Exit* FERANDO.)

   Bian. Delightful, too : Love flies, nor looks before;
I see my father : Yes, there 's something more!
                              (*Going.*   JERONIMO *advances.*)
Another troublesome nothing!   (*Aside.*)

   Jer.   Lady fair,
Pardon whatever in my speech seems rude,
And in thy mirror see my argument,
As in my heart—thy loveliness.   O hear me,   (*Kneels.*)
Though I am low, and dignity is thine,
May love not raise me?   (*Aside*)—to a *golden* power!—
Answer, and bless me with thy answer, lady,
And thy devoted slave I am forever!

Bian. Rise.   I do not seek a slave !   A man
Should be a free man !   (*Aside.*)   What a love is this !
Itself disgraced, and would disgrace a woman !
   Jer. I cannot rise, till in a gentler tone
Thou bid'st me.
   Bian.   Then forever rest thee there !
Thy body's attitude becomes thy mind,
Stooping to degradation !   Go, sir, go !
   Jer.   (*Rising and grasping her arm.*)   Not till I have
      my answer !

(BIANCA *screams.*   JERONIMO *releases her, and is retreating, when he meets* NINA.)

   Nina. Why, what's the matter ?   Is my lady harmed ?
   Jer. Not in the least.   It was a snake in the grass.
   Bian. (*Aside.*)   'T was truly so.   Nina, my dear, 't is
      well.
Are all things ready for the festival ?
See ! Yonder comes the moon.
   Nina.   To light the guests.
All things are ready.
   Bian.   So : I must receive them.
Come, Nina.   [*Exeunt.*]
   Jer.   Scorned—insulted !   No hope there !
But gold and beauty still are worth the wooing.
She knows me not, but, by the Saints, she shall !
Wake, plotting devils of the heart and brain ;
Quick to the task !   Short time, and much to gain !
                                        [*Exit.*]

21

Scene III.—*Night. A grand apartment in the Palace of Vincenti.* Vincenti *seated at a table, on which his head rests; he sleeps. Gay music heard at a distance. Presently, he starts, raises his hands on high, then, gradually, lowers them.*

Vin. 'Twas but a dream!   Methought the olden fable
Of Jupiter was acted o'er again :
The heavens did open, and a shower of gold
Descended on me!   'Twas a silly dream—
Yet wondrous sweet!   My daughter's festival,
Her eighteenth birth-day.   Rank, and wealth, and beauty,
The proudest, fairest of all Italy,
Come thronging now, with only one ambition :
To please the Goldsmith!   Ha! ha! ha! Vincenti,
'Tis thus thine industry, thy skill in trade,
Thy careful application, are rewarded!
Others must thank their ancestors, but thou—
Only thyself!   It is alone thy merit!
(Walks the apartment proudly.)

Enter Jeronimo.

Vin. What would Jeronimo?
Jer.   I scarcely know—
I cannot speak my thought—but strangely now,
Amid the splendor of thy entertainment,
I think—thy bounty, raising me from earth,
Hath filled my heart with gratitude, encouraged
My spirit even to imitate thine own,
Humbly and distantly, for who may stand,
Seignior, on such an eminence as thou !
Vin. If thus I stand, 'twas toil that gained the place,
The toil, Jeronimo, of many years.
And who shall say I have not well deserved !

Jer. All this, and more!   Thy present honored guests
Declare as much, and prophesy the future.
O pride! how weak and easily-pleased is pride!   (*Aside.*)
   Vin. Prosperity, which makes so many blind,
Gives me new power of sight.   I look afar,
Mine eyes surveying many a foreign shore,
Tracing most secret causes, thence deducing
Wealth and renown for Padua.   Then I see
Also the merit of my faithful clerk :
Much hast thou done, Jeronimo!
   Jer.   And thou,
Thou hast done all for me.
   Vin.   But little yet :
More shall I do anon.
   Jer.   My humble thanks!
   Vin. What can I, even now?
   Jer.   All men have dreams,
And many dream such grand and happy things
As Earth, perchance, may never realize.
For me : Angelic visions visit me,
Not only in the night, but all day long;
Making the world so sweet and beautiful—
All flowers—all music—all—an idle dream!
For then I wake, to scorn my silly self,
That thus am fancy's fool!
   Vin.   Thou art in love!
   Jer. And hopeless!
   Vin.   Then it is the *star* of Venus,
And not *herself* thou lovest!
   Jer.   'Tis a maid.
   Vin. Of human form and blood?
   Jer.   Human and heavenly!

Vin. And canst not win her?   Why, thou art a man:
Well-featured, with a quick, expressive eye;
Gay-robed; and young: and with a low-toned voice,
To steal into the heart!   And canst not win her?
What, then, is wanting?   Gold?   I'll give it thee!
She shall be thine!

 Jer.   Thou hast, indeed, the power.

 Vin. Good!   Have I so?   I'll see what mortal maid,
Or mortal man, will dare gainsay Vincenti!
Methinks I *have* observed thy moody looks,
Yes, for a month past.   Ha! that love! love! love!

 Jer. A dainty damsel, and a rich old father!   (*Aside.*)

 Vin. But tell me now her name!

 Jer.   Thy kindness, Seignior,
Imboldens me to speak: It is Bianca.

 Vin. The name my daughter bears.

 Jer.   It is—thy daughter.

 Vin. My daughter!   Hast thou spoken this to her?

 Jer. I have.

 Vin.   Her answer?

 Jer.   Not a loving one;
But still——

 Vin. No more!   Thou mean and cringing dog!
I found thee, beggared, in the filthy street,
I fed and clothed thee, when thy drunken father
Went reeling 'mid the pointing, laughing crowd;
When she who gave thee birth forsook her cub,
And sold her fame to midnight revellers!
I took thee home, and sought to raise thy life
Above its destiny: All this for pity!
What insolent presumption!   Hence!   Begone!

 Jer. I go.   But lofty heads perchance may fall!
         [*Aside.   Exit.*]

VINCENTI, *after walking the apartment angrily, sits down, and becomes more calm.*
Enter FERANDO *and* BIANCA.

Bian. Father, we miss thy kindly smile, to cheer us
Amid the dance.   Art weary of our mirth?
   Vin. No, my dear child.   The crowd, the sultry eve,
Awhile oppressed me, so I sought the breeze
That plays around our balcony; and then
Came here to rest, where slumber stole upon me.
But I 'll return.
   Fer. The smiling presence of a generous host
Makes doubly glad the bosoms of his guests.
In truth, good Seignior, pleasure fast was ebbing,
As, one by one, the noble company
Spoke of Vincenti absent, asking each:
" Why lingers he?"
   Vin.   I thank them all; and now——
   Fer. Pardon a moment, Seignior.   May I hope
An opportunity to speak with thee
Of that which moves me deeply——
   Vin.   Certainly:
I 'll hear thee now, with pleasure.
   Bian.   I 'll retire.
   Fer. No.   Pray remain, Bianca.
Seignior Vincenti, I would speak of *her.*
With all sincerity, I love thy daughter,
Have told her of my love, and she——
   Vin.   Bianca?
   Bian. Forgive me, father, if——
   Vin.   Thy heart was stolen,
And I not warned to watch it?   Ha! I see!
[*To Ferando.*] I do approve thee, having known thy truth,
Having observed Bianca's preference.
   21*

One reservation must I make withal :
That yet ye tarry but a few weeks more,
A month or so, then have ye full consent.
   Fer. Seignior, my heart's best gratitude and duty !
   Bian. Father, thou knowest mine were always given :
They shall continue.   Life hath been to me
A glittering dream !   (*Aside.*)   I wake in Paradise !
   Vin. Thy happiness is still mine own, my child.
And now the reason that I ask delay :
My brother comes anon to Padua ;
I wish him present.
   Fer.   Willingly we wait.
   Vin. Doubtful, for Love but illy brooks the curb !
                                (*Aside.*)

Ye cunning little imps !   And thought ye, then,
I could not see ?   That all this mighty work
Went on in darkness ?   No, no, no; Vincenti
Hath eyes—believe it !   Even hath a heart
Not yet too cold for love !   Nay, do not smile !
I go no more a-wooing !   Padua
Shall be my only mistress !   I will crown her
Empress of Italy !   I'm busy ! busy !—
And love, they say, thrives best in idleness !—
Let us go in :—but see, our friends are here !

Enter the COMPANY.

And sunshine with them !   Music once again !   (*Music.*)
A moving melody : What think ye, friends ?
These snows are light : even I can tread a measure.
                                 [*Exeunt.*]

ACT II.

SCENE I.—*A street.   Enter* JACOBO *and* TRANIO.

Tra. Friendship is true : perhaps there's truth in love !
I 've only spent three days in Padua,
Yet am I well provided for already !
A place that suits my talent, fills my wish !
   Jac. My rich reward is—Tranio is content !
   Tra. You shall have other.   Friendship is so rare
In this cold world of ours ;
It should not go without its proper meed,
The ardent words of gratitude, that all
May see its beauty, learn to imitate !
   Jac. No more of this, my friend :
¶I only did what you would do for me.
   Tra. I would so, truly.   See, we come again
Before Vincenti's dwelling.   I have thought,
Over and over, what a happy man !
   Jac. He is not happy now !
   Tra.   And why ?
   Jac.   A change
Has fallen on him ; why, in sooth, I know not :
But this I know : When yesterday I called,
On business from Guisseppe, round the door
Were five or six who waited.
They spoke severely of Vincenti, one
With threats of law :
Another, that he would recall his trust

Immediately, and claim a full account.
As yet, my lord Guisseppe doubts him not.
To me the whole affair is mystery.
But yonder comes he now.　Is that man happy?

(*They retire back the stage.*)

Enter VINCENTI, *slowly and musingly.*

 Vin. Am I not rich as ever?　Who can say
I have defrauded him?　Not one!　Do any
Demand their payment twice of me?　Not one!
What, then, can be the cause?　I walk the street,
And those who nearly kissed the ground before,
Now stare me in the face, and proudly pass!
The noble guests whom late I entertained,
Strangely forget me now!　Have I the plague?
Is all my house infected, that they shun me?
The office of the Treasury of Padua,
For which I stood the first in nomination,
Is given to a man less rich by thousands!
What is the cause?　Shall I be ruined thus,
Nor know the reason?　　　　(*Reflects.*)
 Jac. Do you envy him?
 Tra.　　　　　　　　　I pity!

Enter GUISSEPPE.

 Guis. Seignior, I grieve to see thee looking sad :
Art thou not well?
 Vin.　　　　　　Yes, well : If health be all!
 Guis. Be of good cheer!　These idle clouds will pass.
And now, if not upon thy private thoughts
Too much intruding, wilt thou grant me leave
To ask a favor of thee?

Vin.   Speak.   I listen.
Favor of him whom all the world doth shun.   (*Aside.*)
  Guis. (*Aside.*)   I'll prove this wide report, if true or
    false.
Can it be possible Vincenti should -
Forget himself?
Seignior Vincenti, for a certain purpose,
I'd place a hundred ducats in thy charge.
I've entered lately in a speculation
Of great extent, and how it may result
Can no one tell.   In case of failure, then,
I would retain this sum.   Wilt keep it for me?
                [*Presenting a bay of gold.*]
  Vin. Right willingly!
  Guis. And now I take my leave.
My time hath many claimants.   When again
We meet, good Seignior, may I find thee cheerful!
Of this I'm certain : I shall find him honest. [*Aside. Exit.*]
  Vin. Well, all is not so dark as I supposed :
Here's one friend left!   Philosophers declare
That he's a happy man who's sure of one!   [*Exit.*]

(JACOBO and TRANIO advance.)

  Tra. And this is all you know?
  Jac.   But this alone.
  Tra. 'Tis very strange!
  Jac.   Yet hither comes a man
Will tell us more, if more there be, or not.
A busy, prying one is Grumio;
Endowed with lynx-like properties, to find
The smallest secret, or, grimalkin-like,
See clearest in the dark.

Enter GRUMIO, *hurriedly, bearing a burden.*

Gru. O, gentlemen! the most wonderful—Your servant,
sir.

(*To Tranio. They bow.*) The most wonderful things
are about town—

Jac. What—what? A crowd of Grumios?

Gru. Dromedaries! (*In a vexed tone.*)

Jac. *They* bear a burden, too, upon the back,
But, as they bear it *willingly*—good lack!
It were not well to call them Grumios.

Gru. Have out your wit : 'Tis seldom out, Heaven knows!

Jac. And that's because 'tis delicate!

Gru.   No doubt!
I fear, too much so : Pray don't let it out!

Jac. True, it were quite as well to keep it home :
'Twould not find yours, even if it went to Rome.

Gru. Mine stays in Padua—good reason, that!
For where the cream is, there will be the cat!

Tra. Have done! have done!

Jac.   Well, Grumio, what's the news?

Gru. Most wonderful! First a whisper came up, just
like a breeze, then it went on, and on, till it grew a storm,
and everybody was howling : " Vincenti! the rich Goldsmith!"

Jac. What of him?

Gru. Are you deaf?

Jac. No, but in Grumio's company there's danger!

Gru. Then you have not heard it! How the Old Goldsmith is said to be a coiner of base money! And truly
so, say I. For isn't he our best workman in gold and
silver? And surely he wouldn't let his talent rust? No,
but use it to some purpose.

Jac. Speak not too fast!   I've always held Vincenti
Honest as any man in Padua.

Gru. And I the same, i'faith, till now.   But do you see
this ducat?   (*Showing a ducat.*)

Jac. Yes, and it is a good one.

Gru. Only copper and silver!   O the scoundrel!   O
the cheat!   And many are about, just like it: all from
Vincenti! O the villain!   That's the way men live in tall
palaces, and dress finely, i'faith, and brave it through the
land!   But "pride goeth before destruction!"   Down
with the cheat!   A copper ducat!

Jac. Still, this is not enough to prove him guilty:
He gave the coin—but did he know 'twas base!

Gru. A Goldsmith, too!   I'll not believe such nonsense!
A villain, again say I! and let him suffer for it!   But
here am I, chatting, and our Captain will away in his ship!
Hold your breath awhile longer, good wind!   *Addio!*
                              [*Exit, in haste.*]

Jac. A busy rogue, yet lazy one, withal.
And, now I think of it, I'm something like him;
For much have I to do, and still neglect it.

Tra. How many love to see a lofty name
Brought down, dishonored, to their own vile level!
To tear, with harpy claws, a character
Which late they praised—

Jac.   No sermons:
You are not paid for those!   I must away.

Tra. And truly so must I; in this direction.
                    [*Exeunt, differently.*]

SCENE II.—*The garden.*   BIANCA *and* VINCENTI *discovered in the distance, seated.*

Bian. Father, thy brow is burning.   Walk with me,
                                   (*They advance.*)
And the cool evening breeze will bring thee peace!
See how the sun, beyond the purple hills,
Goes down in glory!   See his parting smile
On the tall trees, which fondly wave farewell!
And, on the church-tower, rising from the vale,
The only bright thing now amid the shadows,
How blessèd is that ray!   The true, good man
Thus stands sublime in brilliancy, and points
Calmly to Heaven, when Earth around grows dark!
   Vin. Beautiful Nature!   Comforter and friend,
When men deceive and fail us!
   Bian.   Mark, again,
Dear father, how the ivy climbs the tower,
Embracing it so lovingly, and struggling
Upward, still upward, with a proud affection,
Till both together share the sacred light,
And smile upon the gloom below!
   Vin.   I see!
My own Bianca, thus art thou!   My ivy,
And must the storm soon tear thee from thy trust,
Strewn wild and withering, and I, alone,
Hopeless, to battle with a world of wrath!
What have I done?   Why falls the cloud on me?
   Bian. Whatever strange mistake hath gone abroad,
Whatever ill may happen thee—I stand
Thy daughter still! ready, yea proud, to bear
The burden with thee!   Thou hast thought me weak—
Behold how strong a thing a daughter's love!

I will do all: and from the peaceful sky
My mother's spirit shall look down, and aid me!
  Vin. (*Embracing her.*) My dear, dear child! But do
               not weep! I feel
Courage and hope! O sorrow! blesséd sorrow!
For teaching me such happiness of love!

Enter GUISSEPPE. BIANCA *retires to the seat.*

  Guis. My friend, how fortunate to find thee home!
The ducats which I gave thee recently,
A sudden want requires of me again.
I would not trouble thee so soon, but I——
  Vin. A grave apology for such a trifle!
The money is thine own. My private drawer
Contains it, as I placed it there, unopened.
Seignior, thou 'lt always find me at thy service.
  Guis. It ever has been so. My thanks, Vincenti,
And equal offer.
  Vin.   Let us, then, go in.
I 'll render thee thy ducats. Come, Bianca;
The evening grows too late: the dew is falling.
                          [*Exeunt.*]

Enter NINA, *back.*

  Nina. There 's my master: he will sit, all alone, for
hours, in one of the great chairs, with his hand *so :*
(*placing hers in a pensive manner :*) frowning; sometimes
with closed eyes. Then will he start up, and stare, as if
he saw a ghost: and next, off he strides, from one end of the
room to the other, faster than my messenger, Grumio, ever
went! There 's my lady: she goes about crying, and takes
up this, and that, and puts it down again, and acts like a

  22

mad girl!—except when she meets her father. Mercy upon my life! what does it all mean! And they such merry folks awhile ago! *(Enter GRUMIO, stealing up behind her.)* If it was n't for——

Gru. Me? What then?

Nina. Master Impertinence!

Gru. Who *would n't* be, seeing such pretty fruit in a garden? *(Touching her cheek, playfully.)*

Nina. Forbidden fruit!

Gru. All the sweeter for that! The kind I like best! Now, now, Nina; you don't mean it, though? *Say* you don't?

Nina. *(Turning away.)* Not I!

Gru. Well, I thought so! You 've told me many a time you loved me? Ha?

Nina. My note-book 's lost: I can't remember it.

Gru. I 'll be your note-book. Let me see: what was the last entry? Sunday, as you were coming from Mass. Then up walked I, in my new doublet, and said: "A sweet morning, sweet one!"

Nina. And I said: "Yes, Master Grumio." A great record, that, for your note-book! How it will astonish the world, some day!

Gru. Don't stop so short! Was there nothing else? Shall I read on?

Nina. As you please.

Gru. So be it! O, I think of something now!

Nina. Indeed!

Gru. Has Vincenti paid you, this quarter?

Nina. What impudence! Who made *you* Lord of the Treasury?

Gru. I ask for a reason; a good reason, dear. We are all the same as one, you know. Any ducats?

Nina. (*Aside.*) What can the man want? Some wild frolic, perhaps? He spends too much that way. Well; I answer, for a good reason, too: that I'll not answer! But, hark ye, Grumio! there's wine——

Gru. Dearest!

Nina. (*Aside.*) I knew it! And if you'll come in with me: softly, now; softly; I'll——

Gru. What an obedient husband I'll be! Never the like on 't! Dearest!

(Looking fondly at her, smacking his lips.)

Nina. Come.

Gru. (*Starting, then stops, takes her hand, and looks mysteriously.*) Noticed anything strange?

Nina. Where?

Gru. In the palace.

Nina. Why?

Gru. Dear little dove! I'll tell you such a story; such a story!

Nina. Nothing strange in *that*, for *you!*

Gru. But it's all true.

Nina. Then it *will* be wonderful!

Gru. Now, now! I' faith, Nina, I leaped not over the wall for nonsense, to-day. The strangest news! Ho!

(Striking his leg.)

Nina. Are you mad?

Gru. Almost! (*Striking his leg again.*) Those confounded mosquitoes! I hid among the rose-bushes, while the old fellows were talking, and the cursèd sharp-bills stung me well for disturbing their slumbers! If that's *sub rosa,* I'll no more on 't.

Nina. Ha! ha! ha! Billing and cooing always go together!

Gru. Don't laugh !　There 's another !
(*Striking his hand.*)

Nina. A glass of wine will do you good.
Gru. So it will, dearest !　(*Smacking his lips.*)
Nina. Softly, then.
Gru. As a mouse !　　　　　　　　　　[*They steal off.*]

Scene III.—*The Court of Justice.　Officers and citizens waiting.　Enter the*
JUDGE.

Judge. (*Aside.*)　We must devise a plan to satisfy
The people's clamor; else is Padua
Scarcely a moment safe.　What plan? what plan?
A serious thought.　Already have I done
Whate'er the law allows: summoned Vincenti,
Administered the solemn oath of wager,
Whereby the party charged may clear his name
By declaration of his innocence—
The which he did : and, thus compelled, I gave
A favorable judgment.　Still the crowd
Exclaims, 'tis perjury !

After a pause, the JUDGE *beckons an* OFFICER, *whispers to him, and Exit* OFFICER.
The JUDGE *ascends to his seat, and opens a book.* BEPPO *and* COSMO *converse apart.*

Bep. What does he mean ?
Cos. Ask the law books yonder !　They can tell as well
as I : though, in good sooth, even if they would, 'twere
hard matter to understand their learnéd language.

Bep. A puzzle for old Nestor himself !　But there's
some cunning device afoot, depend on't !　A bright man
is our Judge !

Cos. Ay, bright as gold !

Bep. I've found it: the Goldsmith! May it not be of *him?*

Cos. Like everything now-a-days. When was there ever heard so much of one man in Padua before?

Bep. When Antonio ran away with the Duke's daughter.

Cos. Less: less! But what think *you* of the Goldsmith?

Bep. That a man who cannot plead poverty as temptation, should doubly suffer the law.

Cos. Right! Give us justice! He has raised his head above all of us! He has lived in luxury and splendor, year after year, on the fruit of his crimes!

Bep. Remember, too, he even sat on the bench of Magistrates!

Cos. I do remember. Now, if law be not made to fence the rich; if its object be the bulwark of all; let him be brought to trial; let him receive the punishment!

Enter GUISSEPPE.

Guis. Most noble Judge, I claim the law's protection!
It is well known the popular voice is up
Against Vincenti; equally well known
That I have held long intercourse with him,
In various matters. He accused of fraud,
The rumor spares not me. It is incumbent
Upon my reputation, this be cleared;
Moreover, that the proper criminal
Stand forth, in sight of all.
The honest praise of men I dearly prize,
And will not sacrifice mine honor lightly!

Judge. Justice and reason speak in thy demand.
Yet will the law require a definite charge,
Sustained by evidence incontrovertible:
Hast thou such evidence?

22*

Guis.   I come prepared.
It grieves my very soul, to blot with crime
A name revered and blest in Padua,
A name that shone so fair through Italy,
A name which I have spoken, day by day,
For many years, with friendship! Yet my own,
And all within our city, now demand it.
Thus urged, I come to thee, most noble Judge,
With a plain story.   Lately I deposited
A hundred ducats in Vincenti's hands,
My secret object but to prove his truth,
Not doubting then : and presently required
My ducats back, under pretence of need.
I tried them.   To my great surprise and grief,
Thirty were base ! Again I saw Vincenti,
Who still, in answer to my words, denied
Knowledge of aught, excepting that he placed them
Within a private drawer, where, all untouched,
They waited my return.   Some angry words
Arose between us : and I left him so.

Judge. It is enough, I grieve to say it is,
To found the charge ; unless—good Seignior, pardon—
It should be said, as thou hast intimated,
Thou art thyself accomplice.

Guis.   What, sir ? I !
Is not *my* character—

Judge. Was not Vincenti's ?

(*Enter* OFFICER, *disguised as a foreign merchant.*)

Officer. (*To Judge.*) My lord, I have obeyed your
order. The amount deposited with the Goldsmith, under
this disguise, has been restored. I gave him good and

marked money : but receive back the greatest part in false coin.

Judge. Arrest him instantly ! Yet stay : come hither.

Bep. Did I not say truly : " A bright man is our Judge !" No chance have villains in Padua now !

Cos. Well, they possessed the city long enough. The death of one will be a terror to all.

Bep. Is the penalty death ?

Cos. Death at the block.

Bep. But Vincenti will not suffer. He may even be innocent at last. In any case, great service has he rendered our city, and therefore may be pardoned.

Cos. Not for innocence, he has none : not for past liberality, that 's forgotten : yet is there one hope.

Bep. What is 't ?

Cos. Gold !

Bep. You suspect our Judge ?

Cos. Hush !

Judge. Seignior, thou stand'st accused of coining,
Or uttering, false coins of Italy.
It is a fearful charge : and full of sorrow,
That one, of age, and wealth, and reputation,
Like thine, must answer it.

Vin.   The accuser lies !
I do deny the charge ! My life denies it !
Have I not dwelt among ye from my youth ?
Received the highest honors of your city ?
Nay, more : the confidence of Italy ?

And who is he, when fortune crowns my age,
What envious, fiendish heart, would torture me,
When I would rest, after my many cares,
Or only strive again for Padua?
I dare ye to the proof!   What evidence?
   Judge. The first——   *(Pointing to Guisseppe.)*
   Vin.   My friend, Guisseppe!
   Guis.   Even I.
To test thine honesty, a hundred ducats
Did I deposit with thee, then reclaimed them;
And thirty of the hundred found I base.
   Vin. And *thou*, Guisseppe!
   Guis. I only state the fact: I found them so.
   Judge. (*To Vincenti.*) And then: an officer, here pres-
       ent, sought thee,
In foreign merchant dress, and gave thee gold,
Claiming it back again in like disguise.
How was it, when restored?   (*To Officer.*)
   Off.   'T was chiefly false.
   Vin. Ay, altogether false!   I swear by Heaven,
I looked not on the gold, but kept it locked,
With care beyond my own!
   Judge.   A moment more.
What further evidence?
   Off.   We searched his palace.
In secret drawers were instruments of coining,
With all materials; large amounts of coin,
Base coin, were found throughout.   And these await
The order of the Court.
   Judge.   Vincenti?
   Vin. I stand within the gathering shade of hell:
Yet am I innocent!

Judge. What proof appears?

Vin. None : I have none that may acquit me here :
But *here,* there is no criminal ! (*Touching his heart.*)

Judge. May HE,
The SOVEREIGN JUDGE, thus also render judgment !
For my poor part, I must pronounce thy guilt.
On Tuesday,.in the Public Square, at noon,
Thou diest !

Enter BIANCA, *wildly.*

Bian. Father ! Father !

(*She sinks at his feet, embracing him, and weeping.*)

The curtain slowly falls.

ACT III.

Scene I.—*Night.   A forest.*   Ferando, *alone.*

Fer. Day has no joy for me, and night no rest;
And day and night shall bear an equal care,
Till from the chaos of this mystery
I bring the light.   'T is now the darkest hour:
The shrouded form of Doom comes nearer still,
And, like a figure in the hovering fog,
With each advancing step is more gigantic !
I must believe Vincenti innocent :
Aid me, O Heaven ! to prove it !   If I fail—
What image rises to my tortured sight !
The silvery hair of age is dark with blood—
A maiden wanders in a whirling storm,
Beating the ruthless winds with maniac arms !
Her shrieks—Have mercy, God !

Enter Florio.

Flo. All through the woods I ran to meet you, sir.
And I had falls, too.   What a lonesome place !
I ran to meet you, sir.
    Fer. (*With indifference.*)   Well—you are here.
    Flo. Thank my young legs for that !   And if they 're
                wounded,
'T is in the service of a dear, good master !

Fer. Who will remember it.   But news—what news?
Hast thou done all I told thee?
Flo.   To the letter.
And such a weight of wonder bring I back,
The marvel is, how I could ever bring it;
Though twice or thrice I fell, too.
Fer.   Quickly, boy!
Flo. Good news!   (*Clapping his hands.*)
Fer.   Ah, that is light!
Flo.   And that's the reason
I rose from every fall, and flew along.
Well, sir, I found the man you sent me to.
A villain, sir—if I 'm a boy—a villain,
With looks that show the sin his heart would hide,
And his arm only do in secret, sir——
Fer. Dwell not upon his looks!
Flo.   They dwell on me—
They haunt me, sir!   I feel I'm not so good
Since *he* looked on me!
Fer. (*Encouragingly*)   Yes, my noble Page.
Proceed.
Flo.   I tried my simple way.   Ah ha! you know it—
And he was caught—but then I pitied him,
And blamed myself, that, in an angel's guise,
Had found the devil out.   His heart grew soft,
And as his head was not unlike his heart,
My doleful story moved him presently.
In brief, my lord, your supposition 's true.
Fer. True! I am glad to hear it.
Flo.   Hear it, then.
This *honest* friend of mine, who, like a mushroom,
Grew in a single night—this sap-head villain—

Is of a goodly company of coiners,
·That chose a cavern here within the wood,
And set a mint up, but forgot the license.
The Chief of this most honorable body
Is a rare hero—though my new-found friend
Esteems him over-rated.   From the picture,
It seems to me I've met His Mightiness,
Even in Padua ; and, to assure me—
I now propose to visit him straightway,
And introduce my master, which to do
I have secured all means.
  Fer.   My gallant boy !
  Flo. My duty, sir, is but begun : your praise
Must not o'erpass it.
  Fer.   Let us on, at once.
I see the gleam of Hope !
  Flo.   I think it shines
From out the crevice of a cavern, sir :
Within, the torch burns full !   The way is short,
But longer than my story.   [*Exeunt.*]

Scene II.—*Interior of a Cave.*   Jeronimo *discovered, counting coins.   Men sleeping on the ground.*

  Jer. The bells have struck the first hour of the day :
O when they strike the central !   Then farewell
Vincenti's glory : welcome my revenge !
Disguised, I've mingled with the citizens,
From day to day, and still the more enjoyed
The working of my plot !   'T is brave ! 't is brave !
Sleep on, ye drunken fools !   Your master wakes !
The angel of his wrath converses with him
In words of fire, not for dull souls like yours !

Love's heaven is now transformed to Hatred's hell,
Peopled with myriad mad and laughing fiends!
Ha! ha! 'tis happiness!

Enter, unobserved, FLORIO and FERANDO.

Flo.   You know him, sir?
Fer. Through all disguise—Jeronimo!
Jer.   And I have done it!
The keys—I have them here: Good keys, my thanks!
This was the pass-word to Vincenti's office,
This to his private drawer—and this—and this—
True gold I got from thence, and false coin left
To fill the place on't: excellent exchange!
   Fer. Villain! (*Draws his sword, advancing.*)
   Flo.   Peace, my lord! not yet! (*Restraining him.*)

(JERONIMO *starts, alarmed at the sound, examines the Cave, and returns to his position.*)

Jer.   Some caitiff there,
Muttering of his debauch.   I grow a coward.
Faint heart, be bold, be bold until the noon,
And then forever!   Ha! to think I did it!
I brought that grand old head, dishonored, down!
I taught humility to proud Bianca!
Yes, 'twas a wise thing, 'twas a very wise one,
To hide my money-making instruments
In old Vincenti's palace! ha! ha! ha!
   Fer. By Heaven, I cannot bear it!   (*Draws.*)
   Flo.   Peace, my lord!
   Jer. And so, a little while, and it is done:
I'll to the Public Square! to see him die!   [*Exit.*]
   Flo. Let us depart, my lord.   'Twere rashness now.
      23

His fellows are around him ; we are two,
Or I am nothing.
  Fer.   Thus far fortunate,
The rest may follow to the happy end.
Come, then, no more my servant—come, my friend!
                                  [*Exeunt.*]

Scene III.—*The Banquet Hall of Vincenti's Palace. Furniture disarranged.*
Enter Jacobo, Tranio, *and* Grumio.

  Jac. The banquet hall !
  Tra.   A sad, deserted one,
An image of its master !
  Gru.   Yes, of him
Who shall have none to-day !
Or, like a broken plaster image—headless !   (*Sings :*)

> "Go on, my good master,
>   But faster, and faster,
> The headsman, he follows, follows !
>   There 'll be a great knock,
>   When block goes to block,
> And the headsman ———"

Out on 't ! I have forgot that rare old song !   (*Sings :*)

> " And the headsman ———"

Don't *you* remember it ? What's next "the headsman?"
  Jac. Is n't it—Grumio ?
  Gru.   Neither rhyme nor reason !
But let it pass. It wants but few hours now,
And up goes Master Executioner,
And down the Goldsmith !
  Tra. (*To Jacobo.*) How I pity him !
He has a daughter, too.
  Jac.   A lovely girl !
It was my fortune to be present here,

The evening of her birth-day festival.
How bright she shone amid the noble throng,
Courted by all.   And then how proud Vincenti,
As her sweet voice arose !   And prouder still,
And happier was Ferando, looking love,
Which she reflected back with smiles and blushes !
By Jupiter !   I scarcely knew myself !
Scarcely remembered me a simple Clerk,
Only admitted by Guisseppe's favor ;
So beautiful and grand was all around !
  Tra. Alas, the change !   'tis pitiful !   O pitiful !
  Gru. I 'd like to know how many sighs you 'd give,
If 'twere a poor man ! I have none for *him*,
A coiner, a mean, contemptible—
I 'll laugh to see his head roll !—
  Tra. Whatever crime a man may suffer for,
He claims our serious pity.   I deny
The right of law in penalty of death,
And most of all for crime not causing death,
As this is.
  Gru. Have a care !   Your wits are failing !
  Tra. I only speak my thought.
  Jac.   What then ?
Shall villains go at large, and do their will ?
  Gru. Answer us that !
  Tra.   Are there no prisons left ?
What mischief can they work behind the bars ?
What good may not ensue from thought and teaching,
If really guilty ?   Then, if innocence,
One day, perchance, be proved—we can restore
Their name and freedom.   Can ye so with him
Whose head is taken ?
  Jac.   Why, a country life

Has set you dreaming : yet there 's truth in dreams ;
Sometimes there 's truth in dreams !   (*Musingly.*)
  Gru.   But none in this.
The law is so, and wise men made it so ;
And so it has been, many good old years ;
And so it 's no affair of mine ; and so
I 'll none on 't !
  Tra.   Bravely argued !
  Gru.   Glad you like it !
But all your words of new-discovered right
Don't touch the Goldsmith.
  Tra.   Do they not ?   Suppose
The sentence be unjust——
  Gru.   I can't suppose it !
  Tra. Then it is dark.   The universal praise
His previous life received ; and, more than all,
His kindness and his liberality
Forbid belief of wrong.   There 's some mistake !
  Jac. Too late to think of it.   His time is near.
  Gru. So near, that if we 'd witness the beheading,
'T were best we swiftly pass along the rooms,
Learn all we can—what splendor once he lived in—
And thank our friends, the officers : then go.
  Tra. For my part, I regret I ever came :
I will not see his death.
  Jac.   Nor I.
  Gru.   The law
Shall have the dignity of my appearance,
Like a true subject.   Shall we on, good Masters ?   [*Exeunt.*]

    Scene IV.—*A cell of the Prison.*   Vincenti *in chains.*   Bianca *weeping.*

  Vin. Be comforted, poor child ! 'Tis nothing—nothing !
I go awhile before—

Only a little while. And *there*—I see
Thy sainted mother looking down to cheer
My parting hour, with promises of joy!
   Bian. So soon! so soon!
   Vin. (*Pointing upward.*) The FATHER OF THE OR-
         PHAN! If the world
Look coldly on thee, still confide in HIM,
Remembering ever—I am innocent!
   Bian. Innocent—and—to die! O cruel Earth!
O pitiless Heaven! for ye behold the wrong,
And will not save!
   Vin.   Be calm. Accuse them not.
Heaven gave prosperity, I proved ungrateful;
Or thanked, in vanity, myself alone.
Then came adversity, to humble me,
And point the proper path. 'T is well: 't is well!
   Bian. O, my dear father, kind wast thou to all!
And kind—*so* kind to me!
   Vin.   I feel, alas!
Much have I left undone: yet humbly trust
Pardon awaits me; not from man: Were GOD
Merciless as HIS creatures, Heaven, indeed,
Were dark as Earth, and hopeless! Still my heart,
Illumed with sacred light, forgiveth all.
And though the law may confiscate my wealth,
True friends will rise to thee, when I am gone,
Like fountains in the desert, moved by GOD!
Ferando——
   Bian. Father!
      (*With agony, throwing herself on his breast.*)
   Vin.   What is this, poor girl!
Alas, I know it! Love's enchanted palace
   23*

Was built upon the sands: the storm hath crushed it!
Yet, from the ruin, build another up,
And found it on the ROCK, and dedicate
Its glorious beauty to the HOLY SPIRIT!
All shall be well!

   Bian.   I feel it would be so;
At least a single ray of blessèd light
Would pierce the darkness;
If this weak, timid heart resembled thine!
O THOU!
Who lookest on my father's dying hour;
Making it valiant, in the face of terror!
Making it cheerful, in the night of sorrow!
Making it trustful, when the angel Hope
Waves her soft wings for flight!
Give strength and courage to an orphan's heart,
To bear whatever ill may now invade;
To smile, and still live on!   (*A distant sound of bells.*)

   Vin.   The hour approaches.
Leave me awhile, Bianca.

   Bian. I cannot, cannot leave thee, father!
                             (*Clinging to him.*)
   Vin. Nay, nay: be resolute! We meet again.

   (*He conducts her to the door, knocks upon it thrice: a bar is removed: and exit*
BIANCA. *The bar replaced.* VINCENTI, *after walking the cell to and fro, sits down,
and hides his face. The music of the "Miserere" faintly and fitfully heard from
the Cathedral. He starts, and listens.*)

   Vin.   Forever, ever sweet!
'T was thus I heard the solemn, sacred tones
In my gay boyhood; and my wild heart grew
So calm and hushed: as if an angel choir
Joined their grand voices in the dim Cathedral!

Yes: " Miserere!" Pity me, O God!
For then came manhood on, and I forgot Thee,
And from Thy Holy Temple turned away,
To worship at the shrine of tempting Gold!
Again, the sweet, sad tones I loved so fondly!
They fall upon my soul with soothing power!
They steal upon it like the dawning day!
Yes: " Miserere!" Pity me, O God!
Methinks it were no pain to die this moment,
The last of earthly sounds—so sweet!—so sweet!—

(Music gradually ceases.)

Scene V.—A street. Enter Nina, weeping.

Nina. My poor, poor Master! And my Mistress! it
will break her heart!

Enter Grumio, singing.

Gru.

"But faster, and faster,
The headsman, he follows, follows!"

What's all this about, Nina?
　Nina. You know! you know!
　Gru. The cheating Goldsmith?
　Nina. Poor, poor man!
　Gru. A rich one too long!
　Nina. And so kind to me!
　Gru. Well, there *is* some truth in that! For I've had
your ducats tried, my dear, and they're all gold. Pity he
did n't pay other folks in the same metal! You shall have
your ducats to-morrow, dear.
　Nina. Don't speak of them, now.

Gru. Why not?

Nina. I can think of nothing now, but—dreadful! dreadful!   And both so kind!   "Do not forget me, Nina!" she said: and her eyes were full of tears. "Take this, my last gift; and keep it, Nina; keep it, for my sake!"   (*Taking a miniature from her bosom, and kissing it repeatedly.*)

Gru. What is't?

Nina. Her own loved face!   And so like her!   Just as she looked, that happy, happy evening!   I *will* keep it.   Yes! till death!   (*Kissing, and about to replace it.*)

Gru. Let me see.

Nina. (*Giving the miniature.*)   Dear lady Bianca!

Gru. Set with diamonds!   Nina, our fortune's made! We'll marry at once!   We'll leave Padua!   We'll commence a snug inn, among the mountains: where the brave Banditti will visit us, sometimes! fine fellows! noble fellows!   The ducats! the diamonds!   That's the life for me!   We'll marry to-day!   We'll——   We'll—— Ducats! diamonds!

Nina. (*Snatching away the miniature.*)   Go!

[*Exit, in anger.*]

Gru. Go!   Gone!   A good riddance, say I!   A fine reward for my love—for the mosquitoes—for——for—— Go!   Well, let her go!   She went without her ducats! Ha! ha!   It must be near noon, by the sun.   (*Sings.*)

"Go on, my good master,
But faster, and faster,
The headsman, he follows, follows!"—

And then comes the crowd!   And a grand show will it be; with waving banners, and shining steel; and men, and boys, and women, running here, running there; and faces in windows, and bending from balconies, and roofs, and towers! A grand show will it be! Strange we don't have more of them! A city nearly full of villains, and hardly once a month do they furnish entertainment for *honest* people! But a great day shall we have now! Never was one like it! The streets are—— (*Bell tolls.*) Halloo! there goes the bell! His big voice sounds oddly. He is hoarse with calling to so many! I never was too late where heads roll! Ha! ha! (*Sings.*)

> "There 'll be a great knock,
> When block goes to block!"

[*Exit, singing.*]

(*Several persons cross hurriedly.*)

SCENE VI.—*The Public Square. In the centre, the Scaffold and Block. Standing near, the* OFFICER. HEADSMAN *resting on his axe. Bell tolling. Slow music from the distance; gradually approaching. It ceases. Enter* VINCENTI, *guarded. Enter* GRUMIO, *and* CROWD. *Enter* JERONIMO, *disguised, and* FLORIO. *Bell ceases.*

Gru. Just in time, i' faith! " 'T were pity to lose any of it," said the cat, when the milk-maid's pitcher tumbled. Here stand I! (*Placing himself in position.*)

(VINCENTI *ascends the Scaffold. His chain is removed.*)

Off. Prepare!
Vin. I am prepared! Nothing remains,
Save to repeat my former declaration.
Before the World, before that AWFUL POWER,
I stand assured : for I am innocent!
And now, O GOD! I do confide to THEE
My Spirit!

(*Throws open his collar. The* HEADSMAN *slightly moves the axe.*

Enter BIANCA.

(*She rushes toward the Scaffold, but is held back, struggling.* VINCENTI *leaps down from the Scaffold.* BIANCA *breaks away, and they meet in each other's arms. They are torn apart.* BIANCA, *being forced in the opposite direction;* VINCENTI *re-conducted to the Scaffold, and in the act of ascending—*)

Enter FERANDO, *disguised.*

Fer. Hold!

(*Presents a paper to the* OFFICER, *who makes a sign to the* HEADSMAN, *arresting the execution: then reads the paper.*)

Gru. What's this! The Judge gets the money, and we miss the show! Rich men can do what they please in Padua! Fie on 't!

(*The characters stand, grouped: all looking to the* OFFICER, *with intense interest.*)

Off. An order from the Court. Vincenti's free!
Fer. The criminal is here!

(*Grasping the arm of* JERONIMO, *and throwing off the disguise, and also discovering himself.* JERONIMO *draws his dagger, but is disarmed.* VINCENTI *gazes around, with bewildered joy.* BIANCA *looks gladly toward* VINCENTI. *They meet, embracing.*)

Bian. My dear, dear father!
Vin.   Child! my child! my angel!

(VINCENTI *and* BIANCA *advance to* FERANDO, *who has left* JERONIMO *in charge of* OFFICERS.)

Vin. Thanks, thanks, my friend! I walk in mystery,
As one in sleep.
Fer.   'T will be a pleasant waking,
But, for awhile, sleep on. You move and live.

Enter JUDGE, *and other characters of the Drama.*

(*They salute* VINCENTI *and* BIANCA. FERANDO *converses apart with* BIANCA.)

Judge. (*To Vincenti.*) May'st thou live happily! I
    ask forgiveness
For all the dreadful wrong that hung above thee!
                   (*Taking his hand.*)
Whatever reparation, friends, is ours,
Most gladly I bestow. Vincenti's honor
And fortune are restored!
Receive him back again to your affection!

The CROWD, *shouting.* Viva Vincenti! To the Prison!
the Prison! Viva Vincenti! Let us have music!

Gru. The performance is postponed, owing to the in-
disposition of the principal actor. We shall have a comedy
now, with music and a marriage; but the tragedy will soon
be represented: when Jeronimo will take the part of the
Goldsmith—supported by his entire company. (*Sings :*)

"Go on, my good master,
But faster, and faster,
The headsman, he follows, follows!"

Fer. (*To Vincenti.*) Seignior and Friend! we have
thee once again!

Vin. I cannot speak my gratitude! The life
Which thou hast saved will prove it!

Bian.   I——for once,
A woman's tongue forgets its eloquence!
I thank thee with my heart!

Vin.   'T was his before!
Say, with thy *hand :* for thus 't will be to-morrow!
How bright the rainbow, Hope, shines out through Sorrow!
              (*Distant rejoicing music.*)

THE
LATHAM PRIZE POEMS,

WITH

AUTHENTIC BIOGRAPHICAL NOTICES,

AND

Various Pertinent and Impertinent Remarks,

BEING

A RELIABLE EXPOSITION OF THE PRESENT CONDITION OF OUR NATIONAL
LITERATURE.

—

EDITED BY

ALEXANDER APOLLO SMITH.

24

TO

THE BANKERS AND BARDS OF AMERICA,

HOPING THAT THEY MAY BECOME BETTER ACQUAINTED WITH EACH OTHER,
TO THEIR MUTUAL ADVANTAGE,

THESE INSPIRATIONS OF GOLD AND GLORY,

"THE LATHAM PRIZE POEMS,"

ARE MOST ADMIRINGLY, AFFECTIONATELY, AND HUMBLY

𝔇𝔢𝔡𝔦𝔠𝔞𝔱𝔢𝔡,

BY THEIR OBEDIENT SERVANT,

THE EDITOR.

HOW THE PRIZE WAS OFFERED.

On the morning of February 12th, in the year 1853, the prosy-political people of WASHINGTON were startled by the following announcement in the *National Intelligencer*. In a few days, it was repeated from State to State, throughout our Union: in a few weeks, the whole World wondered!

ENCOURAGEMENT TO AMERICAN POETIC TALENT!

$500 PREMIUM!

IMPRESSED as I am with the controlling influence which is exercised by the fine arts upon the direction and destiny of human affairs, it has given me infinite pleasure to witness the bountiful manner in which, from time to time, painting and statuary have been encouraged and rewarded by the Councils of the Nation.

But, while this acknowledgment is due to the discerning and worthy patrons of these noble arts, it is an equal source of humiliation and sorrow to behold the apparent apathy and indifference with which they seem to regard the incomparably more valuable creations of poetry.

To see them adorn the walls of the Capitol with the glowing revelations of the pencil, and decorate the public grounds with the costly *chef d'œuvres* of the chisel, is an omen of good which will be hailed and applauded by all as a cheering pledge of the progress of refinement. But, whilst they lavish their thousands upon these immobile products of canvas and marble and bronze, they offer no reward for the more exalted, more enduring and renowned ovations of the pen. No fostering hand from these high places has ever yet invited the Promethean fire of poetry to animate the history of our country, which, with all its harmony of form and wonder of proportion, lies asleep around the humble vault of Mount Vernon, ready to spring into life and beauty at the first kindling touch of this genial inspiration.

It surely were a work of supererogation to introduce the proofs that crowd the records of the past to show how far above all others stands the "divine art" of poesy. What are all the paintings, statues, and regalia of Versailles, of Fontainbleau, and the Tuileries, compared with the "Marseilles Hymn?" What

24*

the kingly panoply of gold and gems heaped up in the Tower of London; what the collections of the Royal Academy, or even the time-hallowed shrines of Westminster Abbey, when compared with the songs of Burns, and Dibden, and Campbell? Or what has the world that we would take in exchange for "Hail Columbia" and the "Star Spangled Banner?" Well might the British statesman exclaim: "Let me but write the ballads of a nation, and I care not who makes its laws."

As far as the living, breathing man is above the cold, insensate marble that is made to represent him; as far as the radiant skies of summer are above the perishable canvas to which the painter has transferred their feeble resemblance, so far is poetry above all other arts that have their mission to console, and elevate, and inspire the immortal mind of man.

In view of these facts, and considering the lamentable paucity of patriotic songs in my distinguished and beloved country, and with the hope of being the humble means of arousing a proper public feeling upon this interesting subject. I have been induced to offer, and do hereby offer, the sum of five hundred dollars as a prize for the best National Poem, Ode, or Epic.

The rules which will govern the payment of this sum are as follows:

1st. I have selected (without consulting them) the following persons to act as judges or arbiters of the prize thus offered, namely:

The President of the United States.

Hon. A. O. P. Nicholson, of Tennessee.

Hon. Charles Sumner, of U. S. Senate.

Hon. R. M. T. Hunter,   do.

Hon. James C. Jones,   do.

Hon. J. R. Chandler, of U. S. House of Representatives.

Hon. Addison White,   do.   do.

Hon. Thomas H. Bayly,   do.   do.

Hon. D. T. Disney,   do.   do.

Hon. John P. Kennedy, Secretary of the Navy.

Dr. John W. C. Evans, of New Jersey.

Dr. Thomas Saunders.

Joseph Gales,
Gen. R. Armstrong, } of the Press.
Dr. G. Bailey,
W. W. Seaton,

Professor Henry, of the Smithsonian Institution.

Wm. Selden, late Treasurer of the United States.

Rev. C. M. Butler, Episcopal Church.

Rev. R. R. Gurley, Presbyterian Church.

Rev. S. S. Rozell, Methodist Episcopal Church.

Rev. Mr. Donelan, Catholic Church.

2d. These gentlemen, or any three of them, are hereby authorized to meet at the Smithsonian Institution, on the second Monday of December next, at such hour as they may appoint, and there proceed to read and examine the various poems which may have been received, and to determine which of them is most meritorious and deserving of the prize. And I hereby bind myself to pay the sum aforementioned forthwith, to whoever they shall present to me as the person who has written within the time prescribed the best National Patriotic Poem, and upon their representation that he or she is an American citizen.

3d. All communications must be sent to me at Washington (post-paid) before the first Monday in December next, with a full and complete conveyance of the copyright to me and my heirs and assigns forever.

4th. I hereby bind and obligate myself to sell the poems thus sent to me as soon as practicable, for the highest price, and to give the proceeds to the poor of the city of Washington.

5th. No poem will be considered as subject to this prize which shall not have been written subsequent to this date, and received before the first Monday in December next.

R. W. LATHAM.

WASHINGTON, *Feb.* 10, 1853.

THE LATHAM PRIZE POEMS.

F. G. H.,

THE author of "Nannie," a poem of great popularity in the City
of New York; of the "Croakers," famous in Frogtown; and "Red
Jacket," pronounced "dem foine" by all gentlemen of the turf,
began his poetical life nearly simultaneously with the natural,
having in baby-hood given utterance to the following wonderful
couplet:

" Papa!
Mamma!"

in which, it will be observed, the rhymes are perfect.   Growing
up to man's estate, and writing some fiery poems, a great capitalist,* in order to save the country from war and ruin, engaged
our bard by a large salary *not* to write poetry.   This engagement
continued several years.   The patriotic millionaire then dying,
F. G. H. presently informs us:

" I now am in the cotton trade,
And sugar line."

But, relapsing into song, business, of course, deserted him.   The
usual fate of genius had now been his, were it not that part of a
magnificent legacy† left him by the capitalist aforesaid yet re-
mained, upon which he retired, has written nothing since, save
the Latham poem, and being a bachelor, is living quite happily.

---

* Jacob John Astore.   † One thousand dollars.—*Printer.*

An uncommon ease pervades his versification, a natural, unstudied flow of language, and a careless playfulness and felicity of jest.

The Banker and the Bard.

BY FITZ-BLUE H.

" AT midnight, in his guarded tent,
    The Turk was dreaming of the hour
When Greece, her knee in suppliance bent,
    Should tremble at his power:
In dreams, through camp and court, he bore
The trophies of a conqueror;
    In dreams his song of triumph heard,
Then wore his monarch's signet ring:
Then pressed that monarch's throne—a king;
As wild his thoughts, and gay of wing,
    As Eden's garden bird."—*Fitz-Green Halleck.*

AT midnight, in his office dim,
    Sat Latham, dreaming of the time
When all the land, inspired by him,
    Should pour the mighty rhyme:
In dreams he saw his countrymen
Enraptured seize the tuneful pen;
    In dreams their " Songs of Freedom" heard;
Then felt himself a glorious thing;
Then pressed Apollo's throne—a king:
So wild his thoughts, he cut the wing
    Of a domestic bird !*

At morning, eloquent and long,
    His " offer" met the nation's eyes;

* This passage is rather obscure, but may be presumed to mean, "he cut a pigeon-wing"—there being a dance so called.—*Editor.*

Large print was clamorous for song:
   Hurra, my boys, a prize !
The news passed on; the bards awoke,
   No more content to dream :
" The prize !" upon their senses broke
Like Ætna's flame through Ætna's smoke:.
They seize the long-neglected lyre,
They light anew its ancient fire,
     They bid its primal glory beam :
On every hill, in every vale,
Uprose the universal gale
     Of " Liberty or Death !"
" Strike—till the last of kings be dead ;
Strike—for the stars above your head ;
Strike—for the Yankee Land ye tread !"
     Gods ! I am out of breath !

They wrote—like Emmons, long, not well ;*
   They filled full many a foolscap sheet,
They finished ; let the Judges tell
   Their undeplored defeat.
In fancy, all their rhymes I saw,
In fancy, heard their proud hurra,
   .When the last word was done,
Then saw each paper careful close,
And knew, with thumb upon my nose,
     Not yet the prize was won !

Come to the contest, Fitz-Blue ! come !
   Come as a giant, when he feels

* For once, our great poet is unjust. The author mentioned certainly wrote much—the " Fredoniad," in ten volumes, being but a small part of his labors— yet he also wrote well, and always on national subjects. It is to be regretted that his illustrious critic has so seldom chosen themes of native land.—*Editor*.

His dinner, well assured he's "some!"
　　And, when the broken seals
Shall break so many hearts, to thee
Five hundred dollars fall in fee!
Come in Bozzaris' battle storm,
Red Jacket's Tuscarora form,
Or like thyself, mild, playful, warm,
　　　　In love with wit, and dance, and wine;
And thou art conqueror—thy name,
Which every school-boy knows is fame,
Shall fill the rival host with shame,
　　　　And Latham's prize be thine!

Now to the country where my songs
　　　　Have mounted like a rocket's light,
My genius, more subdued, belongs;
And all her Revolution wrongs
　　　　I'll brand, and glorify her right!
Come, ye who would oppress your race—
Come, who possess an honest face—
　　　　Come to the land of freedom; here
Did tyrants wield their dastard power,
But taught ere long to cringe and cower,
　　　　Hence fled they in their abject fear!
To-day our land is glorious, free!
A people wonderful are we!
To-day our doors are open wide,
Come all the world, and we'll provide
　　　　Room, peace, and joy, and all good things!
Here stars and stripes are sure defence;
Here gold abounds and common sense;
　　　　Here changeful Fitz-Blue sings!

And Latham! with the heroes old
  Of Bladensburgh's historic time—
A moving history—I 'm bold
  To give thee praise sublime!
Like them thou lov'st " our city"—so,
    In danger's hour, would'st cry, " away!"
    Nor heed whoever answered, " stay!"
Nor look behind, once turned to go!
Like them, dost thou in centre stand,
With eyes of love on all the land—
But there hast thou superior power;
On thee has fallen a golden shower,
And liberal art thou again,
Scattering far thy precious rain;
Especially art free to those
Who pretty poetry compose;
Most free when native bard devotes
His lyre to patriotic notes;
And were it not for thee, my friend,
This poem, (now so near its end,)
To freedom's loss, had not been penned!
    'T is done; and in the ages dim,
For many centuries, 't will dwell
In million minds, and men shall tell—
    " It were not written but for him!"
And thus at once our country's praise,
As well as own, in future days,
    Twin stars, shall shine on high!
The Song is Freedom's, we are Fame's;
Two of the few immortal names
    That were not born to die!
25

W. C. B.

SEVERAL sentimental and philosophical poems, some with very hard names, have given W. C. B. a wide reputation, insomuch that he is known from our Atlantic shores almost to the Pacific. He wooed the muse before he had attained his "teens," like Pope, Tasso, Chatterton, and Cowley, far surpassing them all, which fact has been attributed to the nature of our glorious institutions. America is singularly adapted to the production of precocious talent. The boys of this country join political processions, sing political songs, (hence our numerous poets,) run with the fire engines, smoke cigars and swear, like men, and hence they are men at a very tender age. The world beholds all this with astonishment, more and more admiring our freedom.

The Doom of the Singers.

BY W. C. B.

"THE melancholy days are come,
  The saddest of the year,
Of wailing winds, and naked woods,
  And meadows brown and sear."—*W. C. Bryant.*

THE grand, romantic days have come,
  The proudest of all time ;
A Banker calls our poets forth,
  And offers cash for rhyme !
Far in the iron-compassed vault,
  'Mid silver, gold, and notes,
I hear him tell the Continent :
  "Prepare to tune your throats !"

A thousand weak-voiced birds reply,
   Who rhyme nor reason know;
The Banker turns away his head,
   Or only says : " So—so !"

Where are the bards, the true old bards,
   That lately stood and sang,
And shamed away to silent gloom
   This now uproarious gang?
Alas, they've learned another trade;
   For though their songs were sweet,
They got no other pay than praise—
   And praise ain't good to eat!
The poet, in these latter times,
   Wants bread—ye give him stones;
Ye wrong him through his toilsome life,
   Then canonize his bones!

And I, had I not printer turned,
   Had perished long ago,
As the flower that only gives its bloom
   To the death-touch of the snow.*
In poetry was found no pay,
   So, politics I sought,
And recently, at auction, I
   A horse and buggy bought!
What's more, one-third the cost I paid,
   And for the other two,
These patriotic Latham notes
   Shall carry me safe through!

* Chrysanthemum. Its budding beauty is often surprised by winter.—*Author*.

O, thou! whoever now thou art,
  That condescend'st to song!
Inspire me to the height of " prize !"
  I fain would "go it strong !"
Ha! ha! I burn! I rave! ha! ha!
  My Country fills my heart!
Throughout this sublimated form
  There is no mortal part!
For is it not enough to make
  An angel of a man,
To sing thy praise, America?
  And as no other can!

Land of unnumbered boats of steam!
  Unnumbered roads of rail!
Land of magnetic telegraphs!
  And baby-jumpers! hail!
Thy empire from the rising sun
  To the setting sun extends!
The world, and all the rest of men,
  Shake hands with thee as friends!
They see, upon thy starry flag,
  A wonder and a sign,
And own, with universal shout—
  That horse and buggy's mine!

N. P. W.

HERE, as generally, N. P. W. gives the reader a sketch of himself, rendering our biographical task unnecessary. He is the poet of refinement—of polite society—an admirable artist—

"To gild refined gold, and paint the lily."

Advance of America.

BY N. P. W.

"THE dust is old upon my 'sandal-shoon.'
And still I am a pilgrim; I have roved
From wild America to Bosphor's waters,
And worshipp'd at innumerable shrines
Of beauty."　　　　　*N. P. Willis.*

LAND of the daring soul!
Thy child who loves thee, though he wander'd long,
Offers the priceless tribute of a song!
　　Not with the maddening bowl,
Not with the drunkard's joy he praises thee,
But reason's bliss, divinest poesie!

　　Thou art the stranger's home!
Those whom oppression from their native shore
Hath banish'd, hither fly, and never more
　　Would from thy Eden roam!
All this is well, if 'twere but men of rank
And title, having money in the bank.
　　25*

        But when the common kind,
Irish and Dutch; who whiskey drink, who smoke
Tobacco vile—ah, me! it does provoke
        The cultivated mind!
A land to Art and Song so passing dear—
There should be none but high-born gentles here!

        Who cannot wear white kid;
Whose handkerchief hath not the breath of flowers;
Who cannot sing, dance, sigh in ladies' bowers;—
        His presence be forbid!
Let us old France and Italy excel:
The soul of living is, in " living well!"

        Such time shall come at last!
'T is almost here; for Luxury, up town,
Begins to pull the frame-made houses down,
        Where gothic mansions vast
Shall like Alladin's rise!   And look ye, too,
What deeds our papers, what our Bankers, do!

        'T is like a lottery: " PRIZE!"
In largest capitals, stands everywhere!
But still the noblest offer I declare
        That which before me lies;
A Patriotic Poem!   May it be
Worthy my native land, and worthy me!

        These " offers" indicate
The land's progressiveness.   There 's nought so fine
On earth as heaven-born poesie! (see mine!)
        Nought helps to make us great
Like poesie!   The world's supremest boast
Is woman—she loves poesie the most!

REV. C. P. C.

The Rev. C. P. C. had the immortal honor of being born in sight of the Capitol of the Nation, and within the District of Columbia. We may imagine how he stood, a child poet, on the wharf of Alexandria, and gazed with large eyes of patriotism on the swelling dome of our Temple of Freedom, dim and soft in the blue distance; how grand thoughts winged the sunny air from that bannered height, and nestled like doves in his young heart, thence to fly forth like eagles over the earth at the call of the magnificent Latham!

His verse is rather of the transcendental order, but frequently, for a little time, rests on the boundary of meaning.

Voice of a Vision.

BY THE REV. C. P. C.

" Amid the watches of the windy night,
A poet sat, and listened to the flow
Of his own changeful thoughts—until there passed
A vision by him, murmuring as it moved,
A wild and mystic lay, to which his thoughts
And pen kept time—and thus the measure ran:/

"All is but as it seems;
The round green earth,
With river and glen;
The din and the mirth
Of the busy, busy men;
The world's great fever
Throbbing forever;
The creed of the sage,
The hope of the age,
All things we cherish,
All that live and all that perish,
These are but inner dreams."—*Rev. C. P. Cranch.*

Amid the howlings of the midnight dogs,
A poet sat, and in himself did rhyme

A patriotic song, for Latham's Prize.
A vision murmured by him, and therein
America was singing, and his pen
Followed the words—and these the words it followed :

America's my name ;
The round earth knows,
On land and on sea,
If it cometh to blows,
How great, how great I be !
The British fever
Cured I forever ;
Down the hill of Bunker,
Like whipt curs they slunk, or
But climbed to its summit,
To find they " could n't come it "—
Which, in fact, is the same.

My great war hurried on,
Past believing ;
The foe had gone,
Making a dismal moan ;
Ha ! for his grieving !
That was a match-light compared to a blaze,
That was a nudge to the waking amaze !
Him I followed fast,
Often him overcast,
Till all my land he found
Wonderful slippery ground,
Then to the ocean fled ;
There he stood daring,
Boasting and swearing :
" Ocean is mine ! " he said.

"Ocean is yours?" said I.
    In my grand scorn I spoke,
    After him as I broke,
    Tossing the wild waves dark
    Madly both sides my bark—
"Ocean is yours, you say?
    Insolent! clear the way!
    'Tis the world's highroad, and
    That shall you understand!"
So, like a thundering Jove,
    Striking his face
    With red disgrace,
I marked thereon the lie;
Then gave his crazy boat an angry shove!

    Later, I caught again
      Red-Coats intruding;
    Bravely I fought again,
      Still the true mood in;
    Short, then, the fight it was,
      Victory was mine,
    Proving how right it was—
      My "right divine!"

    Later yet, Mexico,
      Largely my debtor,
    Saucy, did vex me so—
      How could I let her?
    Straight I went at her, then,
      Took every town,
    Settled the matter, then,
      Knocking her down!

Thus is it ever, too;
   When, in my wrath,
Nations endeavor to
   Slip from my path!
But if they mind themselves,
   Let me alone,
Truly they'll find themselves
   Ready to own
Amor est sirenus,
   Divine as the stars;
My friendship is Venus,
   My anger is Mars!

Thus sang America, and made the poet
Most happy with her changeful melodies,
And confident, as he had followed them
Faithful with pen, his labor meet reward
Should find in grateful hearts, and Latham's Prize.

G. P. M.

HERE we have the best song of the great song-writer, G. P. M. His ballad of the fair maiden, whom somebody loved, and treated savagely, so that, after suffering through an entire winter night,

> " Her heart and morning broke together,
> In the storm"—

was nothing to this production, though the former received shouts of applause whenever sung. But "The Disunionist" breathes a sentiment dear to the heart of every American, and is therefore destined to an unbounded popularity. This popularity will be increased by the fact that our Bard is a Brigadier-General, uniting with his song-talent the all-conquering power of Alexander, Cæsar, Napoleon, and Bombastes Furioso.

The Disunionist.

BY G. P. M.

> "WOODMAN, spare that tree!
> Touch not a single bough!
> In youth it shelter'd me,
> And I'll protect it now.
> 'Twas my forefather's hand
> That placed it near his cot,
> There, woodman, let it stand,
> Thy axe shall harm it not!"—*George P. Morris.*

MISTER, spare our States!
 Speak not another word!
The silly parrot prates,
 But you're a sillier bird.
'Twas our forefathers' hand
 That fixed our glorious lot,
Then, Mister, let 'em stand,
 I tell you, touch 'em not!

The old familiar name,
   Whose glory and renown
Made England's lion tame—
   Her "meteor flag" come down!—
Mister, hush your tongue!
   Cut not our Heaven-bound ties;
Long after you are hung
   Our stars shall "flout the skies!"

When but a little boy,—
   Blue jacket, pretty pants—
How oft I heard with joy
   My uncles and my aunts,
My father, mother tell
   The greatness of our land—
These foolish tears will swell—
   But*————let our old States stand!

My heart-strings round 'em cling—
   So mind your eye, my friend!
A Brigadier may bring
   Your swaggering to an end!†
Old States! "the free and brave!"
   Here, Mister, leave the spot;
While I 've a sword to save,
   I tell you, touch 'em not!

* At this pause the handkerchief is produced and applied to the eyes. It contributes strongly to the pathos.

† The hundred thousand readers of the "Journal," published in New York by N. P. W. and myself, have been frequently informed, through my partner, that I have the honor of being a Brigadier General in the Militia of that State. I beg leave to repeat the information here, for the advantage of those, if any, who may thus far be ignorant of "mine office."—*Author.*

Mrs. S. J. H.

We regret our inability to give more than a single specimen of our female aspirants for the Latham Prize. They were numerous. Every "Boarding School for Young Ladies" contributed at least twenty. Yet we have been able to prevail only with the present authoress to allow this introduction to the public.

Mrs. S. J. II. is a veteran in literature. We trust she will pardon the word, which intimates age, as, with all the world, we proudly testify to her yet-blooming charms of person.

Her writings, like her manners, possess a juvenile elegance. She is a model for the daughters of the land, in propriety of deportment, and the winning graces of mental supremacy.

The Prize.

BY MRS. S. J. H.

"'It snows!' cries the school-boy, 'Hurra!' and his shout
    Is ringing through parlor and hall,
While swift as the wing of a swallow, he's out,
    And his playmates have answered his call;
It makes the heart leap but to witness their joy,
    Proud wealth has no pleasures, I trow,
Like the rapture that throbs in the pulse of the boy,
    As he gathers his treasures of snow;
Then lay not the trappings of gold on thine heirs,
While health, and the riches of nature, are theirs."—*Mrs. S. J. Hale.*

"The prize!" cries the poet, "Hurra!" and his rhyme
    He readeth through parlor and hall,
Then up to the chambers his summons doth climb,
    And down to the kitchen doth fall;
It makes his heart glad when he utters aloud
    The rhymes to his household, I trow,

26

And he hears, when they praise, the applause of the crowd,
  That shall give him 500, you know!
Let him rest in that hope till the winter shall come,
And then let him shout, or thereafter be dumb!

"The prize!" cries the Poetess (author hereof,)
  " For telling how Freedom I love?
My answer is silence! Go on! Ye may scoff,*
  But my passion all words is above!
When the daughters of Lear were assembled to tell
  How fond were their hearts to their sire,
There were two who spoke fluently, fully, and well,
  But the third, with few words, must retire :—
Should the crown have been hers? Soon the winter will come,
      will come,
And then shall we know who shall shout, or be dumb!"

O. W. H.

Pills and poetry seem congenial; identical, indeed, as it is generally admitted that "Poetry is a drug in the market." O. W. H. is entitled to M. D. after his name, as well as some others in our book. But should anybody imagine for him a character like that in the song :

——— " The Doctor came,
With long face like a Quaker"—

It won't do, for never was jollier man than the Doctor. His

* The first half of this line is, alone, sufficient to prove her a remarkable woman.—*Editor*.

oldest friend hasn't once seen him sad, or heard him sigh. His life is a laugh. All his verses laugh, and make every reader laugh also. Every fat man is lover true of O. W. H. If thin men all knew him, there would soon be no thin men.

The present subject is the most serious he has ever treated, but even here the attentive reader will discover lurking fun, in the jerking style of expression, and in the peculiar construction of the poem.

We need not wish the Doctor a long life; that's certain, because he is a merry Doctor; nor fortune, for he has it; and, therefore, only entreat him to write a National Song every year during the next century.

Our Yankee Land.

BY O. W. H., M. D.

"I saw him once before,
As he passed by the door,
　　And again
The pavement stones resound,
As he totters o'er the ground,
　　With his cane."—*O. W. Holmes, M. D.*

Our Yankee Land is blest!
'T is the wonder of the West!
　　And I think,
On the whole broad earth outspread,
Ne'er so worthily were shed
　　Blood and ink!

For our heroes of the sword,
They did, upon my word,
　　Nobly fight!
And our heroes of the pen,
Both the women and the men,
　　How they write!

I need not now go back
O'er the long historic track,
    This to show;
'T is easy, but, indeed,
As all of us can read,
    Why, we know!

What the Chinamen declare
Of the Tea Land over there,
    Here is true,
That the light of earth is ours,
All the sense, and other powers,
    Old and new!

No invention, but we claim,
Nor action worthy fame—
    But our own!
We shine as does the sun,
For the world to gaze upon,
    Grand, alone!

Then hail the "stripes and stars,"
And the telegraph, and cars!
    And the boat!
Let creation understand,
We're by far the greatest land
    That's afloat!

G. H.

THIS spirited author is no relation of Bunker H., so famed in the early part of our Revolution. Bunker H. was not a poet, though the cause of much poetry : *see* Emmons. G. H. *is* a poet. He has seen the sea. He has stood among the "Ruins of Athens." Byron and G. H. have made immortal both the ocean and that antique-templed shore. And Byron and G. H. are much alike, in caring *not a song* for their native land, and devoting many songs to foreign lands. How G. H. came to write the present National Song, nobody knows. But men, and especially poets, will sometimes do strange things—for money.

Liberty's Jubilee.

BY G. H.

"A glorious tree is the old grey oak :
 He has stood for a thousand years,
  Has stood and frown'd
  On the trees around,
 Like a king among his peers;
As round their king they stand, so now,
 When the flowers their pale leaves fold,
The tall trees round him stand, array'd
 In their robes of purple and gold."—*G. Hill.*

A glorious land, the United States;
 It has stood for seventy years,
  Has stood and found
  In the nations round
 No argument for fears;
26*

Though each had something to say, at first,
  How it could n't live to be old,
That the people free are like tigers loose,
  And apt to be overbold !

    We have pass'd the time
    Of nursery rhyme,
Though yet are we scarce a man,
    But we mean to live,
    And a lesson give
To the world that no other can ;
We will show the world what freedom is,
  (The sweetest of orderly things,)
And prove, by our new arithmetic :
  One President's fifty kings !

And we hope, in the course of a century,
  Living and acting thus,
    From pole to pole
    Shall a voice up-roll
In Liberty's song with us,
    And the farthest shore
    Shall cry " encore !"
And still shall the strain prolong,
    And that Jubilee
    Of a whole world free
Shall end with a " Latham Song !"

C. S.

THOUGH these initials appear in another part of our collection, this poet is not the other poet.   C. S. has published a little book. His poems have illuminated newspapers, shining resplendently among advertisements.   Patriotic subjects have a great charm for him.

America's Battle Song.

BY C. S.

" ARM for the Texan battle,
　　Sons of the brave and free !
Away, and win a soldier's grave,
　　Or a glorious victory;
Cries of your murdered brothers,
　　On the red Alamo slain,
Are pealing in your hearts for aid,
　　And shall they call in vain ?
　　　　Then arm for the Texan battle."—*C. Soran.*

ARM for the mighty battle,
　　Whatever boys ye be !
Wherever born, ye 're brothers now,
　　And lo ! your Mother's ME !
The tyrant rules too many lands—
　　We 'll break his rod and chain !
The world is crying out for help—
　　And shall she cry in vain ?
　　　　Then arm for the mighty battle !

In our destiny is writ:
　　" Ye shall possess the world !"

From shore to shore our stars and stripes
  Unconquered be unfurled !
The Eagle bears our flag,
  The Eagle, bird of Jove :
Let's on, wherever Earth is green,
  And blue the skies above!
    Then arm for the mighty battle !

Shout " Yankee Doodle ! March !"
  And imitate your sires !
Subdue creation, open schools,
  Light Independence fires;
Set all the heavens ablaze
  With rockets as ye run,
And pile a monument of thrones
  To honor Washing—ton !
    Then arm for the mighty battle !

~~~~~~~~~~~~~~~~~~~~~

S. A. E.

Born in the shadow of the Capitol, and now protected beneath
its wings, S. A. E., skilled in the " art divine," were ungrateful
indeed had he not written *several* National Songs.   Yea, he hath
done all this, and more.   For, in early days, he freely gave the
aid of his brilliant pen, and best types, (being a printer,) to aid
a poet who then wandered in the Political Metropolis quite alone,
and, otherwise, quite unfriended.   Thus the subject of this notice
brought forward to the admiration of the whole country a Bard
~~~~~~~~~~~~~~~~~~~~~

who sang its Navy Yards, its Land and Marine Battles, its New-Year Odes, and everything that was——*its.**

S. A. E. has never published a volume of his own poetry, except by recitations on public occasions.

The City of Congress.

Air—"O what is our great-men's commotion."

BY S. A. E.

" YE sons of Columbia, who glory
    At Liberty's banner unfurl'd,
While prizing her " eagles" before ye,
    Their moral send over the world!
Chorus—Let " Liberty" long be our motto,
      And high may her bright banner wave ;
      And he who don't value her blessings,
      Deserves to be spurn'd as a slave !"—*S. A. Elliot.*

YE sons of the Muses, who glory
    At Latham's 500 unroll'd,
Be still !—for a Bard is before ye,
    Who sang in the good days of old !
Chorus—Let Latham count over his money,
      And not a word further be said ;
      A light lingers yet in the District,
      The ivy-crown's green on my head.

Then listen, thou sun, and thou moon !
    Then listen, ye stars of the sky !
Ye hemispheres, Eastern and Western,
    Attend !—for the singer is I !
      [Chorus, &c.]

* We are informed, by the oldest inhabitant, that there was once a Bard in Washington who did all these things, but whose name is now forgotten!—*Printer.*

A beautiful place we inhabit!
  Supremely is Washington fair!
Our Congress is mighty in wisdom,
  You 'd think the old Romans were there!
    [Chorus, &c.]

Demosthenes, hearing himself
  Make speeches beside the loud sea,
Could he listen to Congress, would stare,
  And speech never more utter he!
    [Chorus, &c.]

If Chesterfield, famous for bows,
  And honey-tones, sweetened by art,
Could hear a debate in the " Hall"—
  He 'd leave, with his hand on his heart!
    [Chorus, &c.]

I 've sung the great City of Congress;
  Thereby may the Nation be known:
And now would I sing of its Latham,
  But Latham—I 'll let him alone!
Chorus—Let Latham count over his money,
        And not a word further be said;
        A light lingers yet in the District,
        The ivy-crown's green on my head!

C. S.

A banker, in England, has been celebrated as a poet; a banker, in America, shall be—or, we should have said, a cashier of a bank. Such is C. S., of the good town of Boston. He has already written many fine things. But the greatest wonder about him is that a poet should discharge, in a faultless manner, the duties of so prosaic a business—thus confuting a venerable opinion of the world's, that poets must always live in the clouds.

C. S. is a very modest man, (we suppose with a bald-head,) mixes but little in society, and was never five miles from his native town. He loves his old books, his old friends; is quiet as a mouse, and domestic as a cat. His style of writing is gentle and classical.

Our Land.

BY C. S.

> " Above the crowd,
> On upward wings could I but fly,
> I 'd bathe in yon bright cloud,
> And seek the stars that gem the sky."—*C. Sprague.*

Beautiful Land!
An Eden, most resembling Heaven!
To Franklin's strong right hand
(Pierce do I mean,) thy power is given.

And long and well,
No doubt, he 'll manage thy affairs;
And future times will tell
The wreath became his curling hairs!*

* " His hair has a curl in it."—*Hawthorne's Life of Pierce.*

History, o'er all,
Shall praise, in his administration,
Latham's 500 call,
Resounding through the Yankee Nation!

Therein were seen,
In prose, thought, language sweet as honey,
Enough to prove, I ween,
He could have rhymed, and saved his money!

Yet, since he will,
Smiling, persist to hold it out,
I'll rhyme myself for 't—still,
With heart submerged in seas of doubt.

Beautiful Land!
(As I began do I begin,)
For warlike heroes grand,
Each born with destiny to win!

Home of the Free!
Our Revolution tumbled down
(Where it shall ever be!)
That blood-gemmed serpent-coil, the crown!

Temple of Truth!
Virtue and Mind are honored here!
Grave age and joyous youth
Speak their full souls, and feel no fear!

Bower of the Fair!
Daughters of freemen, giving birth
To others, who shall bear
Still, and for aye, the pride of earth!

J. R. L.

WE have not much to say about J. R. L., because we know very little. He is a handsome young man, (married, ladies!) and a native of Boston.   Leaving law for poetry, he has, strange to relate, "made something" by it; but that's in New England, where most of the people can read.   His life passes quietly, in a half dream of philosophy, somewhat mysterious, yet, so far as we may understand it, good and ennobling.   The thoughtful, hopeful character of our young bard is prominently exhibited in his prize poem.

How and What.

BY J. R. L.

"THERE came a youth upon the earth
   Some thousand years ago,
Whose slender hands were nothing worth,
   Whether to plough, or reap, or sow."—*J. R. Lowell.*

ON famous "old Virginia's shore,"
   Some twenty years ago,
Stood a poor boy, who stands no more
   To dread the wind, or rain, or snow.

But then, e'en then, sublimest thought
   Found room within his brain,
And eagerly thenceforth he sought
   His joy-dream's golden truth to gain.

27

He won it : and to-day appears
  His " prize " in papers all ;
Throughout the land each poet hears,
  And arms him for the glorious call.

Strange that the child of poverty
  Should muse, with downcast eyes :
" My Country; were I rich for thee !
  O, but I 'd give a mighty prize !—

One that should wake the poets up,
  Like battle, rousing Mars !
And every heart's o'erflowing cup
  Should pledge Young Freedom's " stripes and
    stars !"

Strange that the generous thought should live,
  (Such thoughts are apt to die,)
Strange, the once-poor, now rich, should give
  Indeed this prize to poetry !

All praise to him who loves so well
  His lovely native land,
Waking for it the " tuneful shell,"
  And voices wondrous sweet and grand !

Among those voices mine shall rise,
  To dignify the theme—
Perhaps to win the luring prize,
  O'er all the multitude supreme !

NATIONAL SONG.

In the beauty of thy youth-time,
    Thou, America, art blest,
For the dreams of countless ages
    They are true! they are possessed!
And the glories of old stories
    Now are living in thy breast!

All the sages' dreams of plenty,
    All the poets' dreams of joy,
All the freedom of their visions,
    Visions day could not destroy,
All the peace, and truth, and grandeur—
    These are thine, my darling boy!*

And forever, still forever,
    Shall thy happiness extend,
And forever, still forever,
    Shalt thou be the poor world's friend,
Till the world shall come unto thee,
    And it sorrows have an end!

* This variation from custom, in "unsexing" America, may be justified in the reader's mind on reflecting how manly is America's character, as proved in the affair of Mexico, &c. A friend to whom these lines were shown hinted that the necessity of rhyme required "boy." To annihilate such a charge, is it not sufficient to say that I have written ten thousand verses?—*The Author.*

Professor H. W. L.

The stately, strange measure of Professor H. W. L. was never more stately and strange than here. The last line, in its obscure hint, is perfectly awful.

Our learned poet has surpassed himself in this Prize Poem—if, indeed, it be altogether his, for, we regret to say, he has sometimes been caught stealing, and has made large gains thereby, of which fact a noted instance may be found in a verse running thus :

> " Art is long, and Time is fleeting,
> And our hearts, though stout and brave,
> Still, like muffled drums, are beating
> Funeral marches to the grave."

Stolen from the German. And so of sundry other verses.

The Scene and the Song.

BY PROFESSOR H. W. L.

> " In the valley of the Pegnitz, where across broad meadow-lands
> Rise the blue Franconian mountains, Nuremberg, the ancient, stands,"
> *Professor H. W. Longfellow.*

In the District of Columbia, famed for fine tobacco-lands,
By the blue Potomac river, Washington, gay city, stands.

Little knows it toil and traffic, little knows it art and song,
Yet its Avenues, in winter, mighty men and women throng.

Then the banner of our nation, on its Capitol unfurled,
Emblems freedom's blood and heaven-light to the wonder-
    looking world ;

And for fifty years that banner, dome and chimney far
    above,
Thus hath emblemed truth and grandeur, peace, and lib-
    erty, and love.

Yet so proudly waved it never as it shall next winter
    wave,
When the prize shall be awarded, prize the liberal Latham
    gave !

Every crimson stripe more crimson, every star shall brighter
    glow,
Joy shall fill the sky above it, joy inspire the crowds below.

Hath not Latham, by his bounty, honored much that
    glorious sign ?
Will not all the crowd be poets—every poet saying
    " mine !"

" Mine the prize !"   Alas, too hopeful !   For the prize is
    only one,
And, a single bard successful, thousands, thousands, are
    undone !

Even now the fates decide it; all discerning hearts and
    eyes
Well may think and well may read it: I alone shall win
    the prize !

I, who write as foreign, native poet, poetess ne'er wrote,
I, who if I fail in fancy, know the tongues, and aptly——
    quote,
    27*

Stealing thoughts as gypsies children, and disguising them,
    until
For my own sweet babes right freely pass they, offspring
    of my quill !

Therefore, who shall dare dispute it, when the ghosts of
    poets old,
Masters of the charmèd lyre, me shall aid to gain the
    gold ?

SONG.

Hail ! hail ! thou starry land !
Thou, in thy armèd hand,
Holdest sublime command,
        Passing the Roman !
'T is not by tyranny
Millions acknowledge thee ;
Love is thy sovereignty—
        Fear's for the foeman !

Gentle and fair art thou !
Peace on thy angel brow,
Bindeth her rainbow now,
        Making thee glorious ;
But when war shouteth loud,
O but thy look is proud !
Erebus-dark the cloud !
        Then thou 'rt uproarious !

World, would'st thou find a friend?
Hither thy footsteps bend;
Freedom's sweet smile will lend
    Light to creation !
World, would'st thou dare a foe?
Give but good cause, and lo !
One that in hate will go
    Deep as ————*

<hr>

W. W.

ANOTHER genius of whom Washington is proud, W. W. has, heretofore, been only celebrated as an Album-Poet; but there were nobler things in him—everybody knew it—everybody said it.   Long has he been persuaded by the girls, each presenting her pretty blank book and smile: "Do write me some verses ! Now do!"—for W. W. is a bachelor, prospering in trade, and fully able to support a wife: but henceforth his country will importune him, when the following song shall be published.   There is poetry in its very title.

Like a brother bard in this collection, W. W. is a great admirer of Burns, without being at all inclined to the wildness of Scotia's favorite.   His couplets invariably end with "O."   There is one important difference between the poets, however.   W. W. contends that "O" is a good rhyme for "O," and will have no

* A strong comparison was probably intended here, but only a long blot is found in the manuscript.   The *Devil* suggests a word, quite familiar to himself, but the poet choosing to leave us in darkness, so let it be.--*Printer*.

other; while Burns, with his usual extravagance, gives us a
rhyme and " O " in the bargain. But W. W. is undoubtedly right.

The Flag of the Free, O.

BY W. W.

> " A rose is charming to the eye,
>   And to the nose in smelling, O,
>   But of her beauty she must fade,
>   And moulder into nothing, O !"—*William Wilson.*

A flag 's a lovely thing to see,
    When hung aloft, and swelling, O ;
Each nation loves a different flag,
    And I have no objection, O.

But all the people of the earth,
    Who come to live among us, O,
Forget the flags that gave them birth,[*]
    And love our own the dearest, O.

Our Eagle, with his mighty wings,
    They see, protects them better, O,
Our silver " stars " are bright with hope,
    Our " stripes " are for the enemy, O !

Then let us swear we 'll make our flag
    As wide as yonder heavens, O,
And like the " stars " that look on us,
    All stars shall look on freemen, O !

---

[*] We cannot otherwise account for this rhyme, in the common acceptation,
than by supposing it inserted by some friend of the Author. Indeed, the manuscript bears us out in the conjecture, as a word has been erased here, and "birth"
seems written by another hand.—*Editor.*

J. E. T.

OF J. E. T., as of Chatterton, might be written:

"The marvellous boy, that perished in his pride,"

only that he has not yet "perished in his pride," but "lives and expatiates" in it, more and more every day. Though still quite young, his works are wonderful, his prose and poetry being alike profound, and, in general, beyond mortal comprehension. He imitates Willis, but has out-Willised Willis.

Trio.

BY J. E. T.

"OF literature, he knows a little—
 That is, of foreign; and whate'er of native
He deems insipid, and to entitle
 It a moment's rank above creative
Things of half-way excellence, is to settle
 A thing that is entirely decisive
With English potentates in literature,
Who rule the realm of letters as of war."—*J. E. Tuel.*

I sing my Country! I who lately sang*
 The "Age of Tinsel," and some other things
Which the world knows of. Their music rang
 Wild as a gong! Thou Eagle! O, what wings

* The first line of this beautiful poem resembles one by Cowper:

"I sing the Sofa! I who lately sang," &c.;

But its dignity is so improved by the introduction of "my country," that we consider the whole fairly original. J. E. T. often thus improves on the productions of his tuneful brethren.—*Editor.*

Hast thou, indeed, and what an awful clang
    Their anger makes, and how it startles kings!
Thou art terrible in war, but in peace the
Lamb itself can not more gentle be!

Great hast thou ever been, my Country, but
    Greater art now than ever, and in my
Opinion all creation cannot put
    Three such great men together as in thy
Happy dominion live at present!   Shut
    Your mouths, ye nations, and attend, while I,
Low-bending, in my verse do name their names:
Latham and Willis, and a third, whose fame's

Green, it is true, but shall be evergreen,
    And likewise glorious!   Who can hesitate
To know, decidedly, the man I mean?
    Yet, from all minds all doubt to dissipate,
Let me proclaim this third.   Him hast thou seen,
    About hotels, in after-dinner state,
If ever thou in Washington did'st stand:
'T is I, myself! This Trio is most grand!

The first hath been the first to offer " Prize"
    For patriotic poem! And the second one
Is quite our best of poets.   His talent lies
    In true refinement, which he hath well done!
And for the third—excuse these modest dyes
    That now my cheek ensanguine round upon—
I imitate great Willis, and do him love
With such affection as the angels do above!

But I wander from my theme, although to stray
  Is not my custom—custom honored more
In breach than the observance—and I pray
  That our fair native land, to farthest shore,
Be happy, and a perfect " milky way"
  Of stars, at last, be hers, and nations o'er
The waters form a part of it, and all
In glory shine, and never, never fall !

JOHN SMITH.

JOHN SMITH is universally known, and respected.　He is an
admirer of Burns, whom he has been accused of imitating, which
accusation he only answers with a laugh and a capital " O."

Sons of Freedom.

BY JOHN SMITH.

" BEHIND yon hills where Lugar flows,
  'Mang moors and mosses many, O,
The wintry sun the day has clos'd,
  And I'll awa' to Nannie, O."—*Burns.*

I'VE dollars in the Latham Bank,
  Good friends, too, if I need 'em, O,
But most of all kind heavens I thank
  That I'm a Son of Freedom, O.

The Yankee boys who gained our rights,
  True Yankee boys succeed 'em, O;
We 're still the very deuce in fights,
  We soldiering Sons of Freedom, O.

We 've took and give enough of blows,
  We 've took, but did n't heed 'em, O,
And please to not tread on our toes,
  We 're peaceful Sons of Freedom, O.

I wish you nations over seas
  Had chased your kings, and treed 'em, O,
You don't know what a life of ease
  Have all the Sons of Freedom, O.

There 's not a lad throughout our land,
  I don't care who may breed him, O,
But has an empire in his hand—
  We ballot-boys of Freedom, O.

God bless the glorious " stripes and stars !"
  Be every good decreed 'em, O,
And wave and shine till all the jars
  Of earth be hushed in Freedom, O.

Song and Self.

BY J. S. K.*

ROMANTIC tale of mount and vale
　　And stream and lake of foreign shore:
By such alone their charms are known,
　　For ne'er I crossed yon ocean o'er;
　　　　Nor have I wish to roam.
Our East sea-strand, our Southern land,
　　And Northern, have I often seen;
Enough of fair, sublime, are there,
　　To fill my soul with joy serene,
　　　　And make me proud of home!

Even upon our poorest soil,
　　Where scarce a tree or bush will grow,
Where, by the long, long days of toil,
　　We scarce win bread—we're prompt to show
　　　　Noblest productions—MEN!
Those who from humblest life up-rise,
　　To shine in Senates, Armies, Bars,
Making the old world ope her eyes,
　　To comprehend our wondrous stars—
　　　　Nor solve the mystery then!

* The envelope containing the full name of this author could not be found,
when his poem was given to the Editor, who, however, supposes it to be *J. S.
Kidney*, of somewhere South.

28

And soon all foreigners shall see
  The glory of our favored time;
America, sweet lass! shall be
  Victorious in the lists of rhyme,
    Beyond Europa's fame!
For this shall all creation thank,
  While ages yet on ages roll,
The Prize bestowed at Latham's Bank,
  By Latham! Music-loving soul!
    Ring out his honored name!

In visits made to Washington—
  For once I had a claim or two;
I wish the Government had done
  Me justice, and had passed them through—
    But let the gone be gone!—
There saw I Latham. 'Twas, I think,
  In Seventh street his Bank was placed.
His long, lean fingers full of ink,
  He wrote a business note in haste,
    And put his beaver on.

Then, striding forth, away he sped,
  And never more we chanced to meet;
But ever in my heart his head,
  His smile, so kind, so boy-like sweet,
    His low-toned voice, will rest;
And equally my pride and joy,
  Through all my life, shall be, to tell
To every woman, man, and boy,
  And every little girl as well,
    How much I was impressed!

Now for the Prize his bounty brings,
  So dazzling, in the nation's sight,
May every bard pluck eagle wings,
    And make a pen therewith, and write :
      And hail to him shall win it!
I care not whom; I only ask
  The song with proper care be done,
That Liberty inspire the task,
    And stars and stripes, and Washington,
      And Latham's name be in it!

SPIRIT-RAPPING POEMS.

Antonio.   Now, by the gods,
Thou dost amaze me!
   Miss Jane.   I 'll amaze thee more!
What ho! (*stamping her foot,*)
From under ground, above, far, near,
        Spirits!
Poets of the Past, appear!
See! a dullard doubter 's here!
        Spirits!
Ope the lap-milk kitten's eyes!
        Spirits, rise!

BOSTING, U. S.

To the Onerable the Judges of the " Latham Pomes."

GENTLEMEN: Imejetly on the publicashun of the Latham prise offher for the best Nashunal Pome, we receved a comunicashun from the Speerit Wurld, distinctly xpressed by "rappins." This comunicashun proseeded from R. M., who lived in this wurld about the yeer 1640. It enformed us that a meetin had just bin helld in the Mysterus Land, when the sed R. M. was called to the cheer, and E. A. P. apinted Secktary. A resolushun was presented by Dr. R. E., and carrid *non compos*, that each member of the meetin (all havin bin Amerikan poets) instantly prepair and transmit a Latham Pome, "not for the prize, which were now useless to us, but to augment the glory of our late and ever-to-be-remembered country."

We reseeved the pomes, which we have the oner to lay befor your oners, each in the undouted hand-ritin of its orther.

That your oners may concent to their publicashun, in book form, with the rest, is the umble prair of

Your Oners'
Umble Sisters and Servents,

THE MISSES WOLF.

P. S. Speeritual comunicashuns attended too promptly and on reesonable turms. Refer to X-Cenitur Tallsage.

E. A. P

IN the following poem we find the familiar peculiarities of E. A. P. still preserved—his repetitions repeated. The cause of these, as we have been informed, originated in youth. His Grandmother, to whom he read his verses, was very deaf. Finally he acquired the habit of writing in this way—which habit was doubtless assisted by his natural inclination for the strange.

Gold-Gift.

BY E. A. P.

"THANK Heaven! the crisis—
The danger, is past,
And the lingering illness
Is over at last—
And the fever, called "Living,"
Is conquer'd at last."—*E. A. Poe.*

THANK Latham! the country
Is happy at last!
His gold to the poets—
Much needed—is cast,
His life-cheering eagles
Are proudly out-cast!

Thousands, I know,
Will exult in their flight;
And our blue-stocking maidens
Will sing at the sight,

And the boys of our colleges
"Spout" at the sight,
And the Nation all over
    Grow mad at the sight!

Now will the universe
    Look to the " stars,"
Now will the prison-doors
    Burst their old bars,
And slaves shall be soldiers,
    And fight with their bars !

This, and this only,
    Was needed to bring
The world to its senses :
    Give gold, and we sing !
And the world, in a moment,
    Is free when we sing !

R. M.

With two other poets, R. M. prepared the first book published in British America. This was "Delectable Stories in Metre, for the Use, Edification, and Comfort of the Chickens of the Colonies, in Public and Private, especially in New England. Printed at Cambridge, 1640."

R. M. acknowledges that he cannot write very smooth poetry ;

"that it is not as elegante as somme may desire and expect;" but claims to have "strong thoughts and common sense—such things being not oft found in poetrie."

Vernon's Mount.

AND HOW IT SHOULD INSPIRE THE LAND.

BY R. M.

> "THE rivers on of Babilon,
>   There when wee did sit downe,
>   Yea, even then, wee mourned when
>   We remembered Sion."—*Richard Mather.*

THE waters nigh Potomac by,
    Vernon's Mount there doth it stand,
Yea, even there, a mansion fair
    Doth woo the eyes of all the Land.

And Washington, great Freedom's son,
    He livéd there full many years,
And freemen they his tomb survey,
    And do it consecrate with tears.

This noble is, and proveth his
    Whole life did to the States belong,
And doth require the muses' fire,
    And eke a patriotic song.

'T is also good that Latham should
    Therefor a mighty prize present,
And I do think vast floods of ink
    And paper will therefor be spent.

Thou mansion old, which I behold
    In fancy, and no otherwise,
Thy gables tall, thy chimneys all,
    Long may they pierce the changing skies!

May Vernon's Mount, on no account,
    Be put in speculators' purse,
May never there the bad repair,
    Themselves to make, and others, worse!

But bounteous store may evermore
    Of highest thoughts thereby be given,
To light our days, and build our praise
    From beauteous Earth to blesséd Heaven!

And may it be the propertie
    Of people Washington has saved!
Yea, ever fast, until the last,
    That sacred place in heart engraved!

Like sun it shine, to cheer, refine,
    To warm to life the loving Land!
Thus tyrant power shall cringe and cower
    Before its deathless influence grand!

Thus hopeful fates shall call new States
    From regions now in vice and woe,
And man's great soul, from pole to pole,
    Shall on in joyous freedom goe!

J. B.

J. B., who is not to be confounded with the character of the same designation in Dickens' "Dombey," was one of our most voluminous poets, having written several epics, each as large as Harpers' Family Bible, or Doctor Johnson's Dictionary. Yet he wrote nobly. His works were remarkable for their unity of fable, their regular succession of incidents, and strong exhibitions of powerful character, thus combining the charms of a narrative. We have not found a single dull passage. We have bent over his ever-changing pages, without intermission, or food, for sixteen days and nights. His similes are particularly appropriate and elegant.

The world admits that his "Columbiad" surpasses the "Illiad," the "Æneid," and "Paradise Lost."

The following production surpasses the "Columbiad:"

Invitation to Song.

BY J. B.

"Through solid curls of smoke, the bursting fires
Climb in tall pyramids above the spires,
Concentring all the winds : whose forces, driven
With equal rage from every point of heaven,
Whirl into conflict, round the scantling pour
The twisting flames, and through the rafters roar,
Suck up the cinders, send them sailing far,
To warn the nations of the raging war ;
Bend high the blazing vortex, swell'd and curl'd,
Careering, brightening o'er the lustred world :
Seas catch the splendour, kindling skies resound,
And fallen structures shake the smouldering ground."

Joel Barlow.

Where Rock-Creek's waters through the vales disport,
And unto George-Town make their tuneful court;

Where trees, and vines, and moss, and wild-flowers grow,
Well pleased to see their mirror'd charms below;
There, oft, when summer's sun was blazing round,
And not a frog went bounding o'er the ground,
I climb'd aloft in some umbrageous oak,
And woo'd the muse, and trembled as she spoke.
Green leaves were over me, on either side,
And far below, and no one me espied,
While fair Columbia in her glory came,
Dazzled my eyes, and set my soul a-flame:
Then, like a blasted rock, burst songs of praise,
And then and there I won my wreath of bays!*
But ah! had Latham in my living lived,
Worthier had been my song, and worthier been receiv'd;
For all discouragements were 'gainst me then,
The plough, loom, anvil dispossess'd the pen,
And deepest mental toil was only said
To prove a lazy, good-for-nothing head!
Had Latham lived—the smile of his regard,
Like love's long, lingering look, had blessed the bard,
Open'd his eyes to joy, his lips to song,
Shot through his heart, roll'd all his veins along!
Regret is useless.   Now I only write
To urge my countrymen exert their might:
Dear brother poets, bless your luckier fate,
Spring early to the task, and labor late;
First read " Columbiad," carefully, quite through,
Which may require a month—not more than two—
Thus shall your minds with thought poetic burn,
When, well prepared, you may to Latham turn,

* I composed the greater part of the " Columbiad" in the branches of an old
oak, on the far-seeing eminence of Kalorama. I found that lofty situation most
favorable to inspiration.—*J. B.*

Catch the sweet smiles that circling gild his face,
Those circling smiles than all mankind embrace,
Tune your wild harps by accents of his tongue,
And sing such songs—as Homer never sung !

R. T. P.

THIS author wrote with a steam-like rapidity. Thought was, with him, a thing of "no consequence"*—a river of rhyme swept away all such little obstacles. Yet he was magnificently paid, receiving fifteen hundred dollars for one short poem, relating to the General Post Office,† and seven hundred and fifty dollars for a song. He resembled a true poet only in one respect, to wit: he was indolent, and, in spite of fortune's favors, poor. His offering is admitted here because it comes in good company.

Latham and Liberty.

BY R. T. P.

"YE sons of Columbia, who bravely have fought
    For those rights, which unstained from your sires had descended,
May you long taste the blessings your valour has bought,
    And your sons reap the soil which their fathers defended.
        'Mid the reign of mild Peace
        May your nation increase,
With the glory of Rome, and the wisdom of Greece;
And ne'er shall the sons of Columbia be slaves
While the earth bears a plant or the sea rolls its waves."—*Robert T. Paine*

YE bards of Columbia, who sweetly have told
    The fame of those fields which your fathers contested,
May your friends be a thousand, a million your gold,
    And your memory in ages unnumbered invested !

* Favorite expression of Mr. Toots.
† Entitled the "Invention of Letters."—*Printer.*

Still to Latham attend,
For the Banker's your friend,
And the sweetest of poems for Latham be penned;
Till Latham's great name with Columbia shall rise,
While there's verse in the land, or a charm in a Prize!

Let the insolent wits of the old world be still,
For now have we books, that are worthy to read, too,
And epics are coming with hearty good will,
And Homer and Milton would own they *succeed*, too!
And the praise shall belong
For the pride of our song,
To the Banker whose money has backed us up strong;
And Latham's great name with Columbia shall rise
While there's verse in the land, or a charm in a Prize!

DR. R. E.

R. E. was both physician and poet. The mortal profession he never practised, but extensively the immortal. So numerous were his Epics that no one has read them (all.) His mode of expression was eminently original, for instance, in one of his Revolutionary poems, wishing to tell us that an old gun rested against a tree, he says:

> "An ancient war-tube 'gainst an oak reclined."

A line the like of which we shall not find in Homer himself!
29

Indeed, throughout the poems of Dr. R. E. we are struck with his Homeric genius, especially in the ingenuity and melody with which he introduces a long list of proper names, like the "catalogue of the ships," in the Iliad.

Gloria Lathame.

BY DR. R. E.

"Howe led the van, with royal star array'd—
Leslie and Pitcarn, next in martial grade;
Richardson, Abercrombie, Williams, Clark,
Percy and Rawdon with a lordly mark;
Bruce, Jordon, Spendlove, Mitchell, Butler, Small,
With whom had Putman wing'd the deadly ball."
Dr. R. Emmons.

Rejoice, O Land, through all thy mighty bounds,
For that no more thou subject art to crowns!
I've sung the perils of thy early days,
And now thy glories perfect claim my praise,
My praise that shall in harmony remain
Till "Hampton's Tincture" cease t' alleviate pain?*

What glorious times the earth doth now enjoy,
I mean that part where I was born, a boy
Romantic, loving verse, that sweet employ!
Yes, my dear Country, happy Country! hail!
How could'st be otherwise, when every gale

* The valuable medicine so poetically introduced in this line is now for sale at the Drug Store of Dr. Patterson, near the market, Washington. It is particularly recommended for—

"The heart-ache, and the thousand natural shocks
That flesh is heir to."
Editor.

Beareth the fame of patriotic songs,
While this to Halleck, that to Sprague belongs,
Longfellow, Willis, Bryant, Cutter, Cranch,
Holmes, Morris, Lowell, Kidney, Tuel staunch,
And other bards renowned, inspired and led
By Latham's self, in old Virginia bred,
Who from " first family" did issue, thence
By slow degrees arose and snug *per cents*,
And now delights in his great offering
Of gold to any native bard will sing !

Honor'd be Latham !   Him shall all men thank,
And bow them at his patriotic bank !
Honor'd be Latham !   May he live full long !
Free flow his notes for fluent notes of song !
And when at last he seeks this shadowy shore,
Deep may his native land his loss deplore,
Which kind Heaven grant unnumber'd Lathams more !

JUDGE H.

THE Rhine Song of Germany, the Marseilles Hymn of France, and the Hail Columbia of the United States! There's glory— with three prongs, like a lightning-rod.

A better patriotic song than Hail Columbia was never written— except the following, in which our Judge is more than sublime.

Pierce and Latham.

BY JUDGE H.

"HAIL Columbia! happy land!
Hail, ye heroes! heaven-born band!
 Who fought and bled in Freedom's cause,
 Who fought and bled in Freedom's cause,
And when the storm of war was gone,
Enjoyed the peace their valor won,
Let independence be our boast,
Ever mindful what it cost;
Ever grateful for the prize,
Let its altar reach the skies.
 Firm—united—let us be,
 Rallying round our Liberty;
 As a band of brothers join'd,
 Peace and safety we shall find."—*Judge Hopkinson.*

HAIL Columbia! happy land!
Franklin Pierce has chief command!
 Who fought and fell* in Mexico,
 Who fought and fell in Mexico,
And when the storm of war was done,
Enjoy'd the place his valor won!

* From his horse.

Now let Franklin be our boast,
Second Washington—almost!
Also Latham and his "Prize!"
Join their names, and let them rise!
  Soldier—banker—let them be
  Rallying words of Liberty;
  Pierce and Latham, wise and strong,
  One for sword, and one for song!

Immortal patriots! rise! behold
Power of steel, and power of gold!
  They win and buy the nations round,
  They win and buy the nations round.
Remembering Pierce in Mexico,
Who now will fear a foreign foe?
Remembering Latham's glorious "Prize,"
What "stripes" will wave, what "stars" will rise!
And both united—who can stand
The swords and songs of such a land?
  Soldier—banker—let them be
  Rallying words of Liberty;
  Pierce and Latham, wise and strong,
  One for sword, and one for song!

29*

HOW THE PRIZE BECAME A BLANK.

On Tuesday, December 20th, 1853, the following appeared in the *National Intelligencer:*

DECISION ON THE PRIZE POEMS.

WASHINGTON, *December* 14, 1853.

SIR: The committee appointed to examine the communications presented for the prize offered by yourself for the best "National Poem, Ode, or Epic," state that they met at the Smithsonian Institution at the time appointed; that, after organization, they directed the names of the authors to be concealed; that, after a deliberate examination, they came to the unanimous conclusion that, in their judgment, there is no production among those submitted of such a character in its conception and execution as justly to entitle it to be considered a "National Poem, Ode, or Epic;" and that they therefore respectfully decline recommending any one of them for the prize.

CHARLES SUMNER,
JOS. R. CHANDLER,
JNO. W. C. EVANS,
TH. J. SAUNDERS,
JOSEPH HENRY,
C. M. BUTLER,
R. R. GURLEY,
JAMES B. DONELAN.

R. W. LATHAM, ESQ., Present.

AND so it is over; and the poets are left lamenting. But no! like true Americans, they appeal from the few to the many, from the Committee to the People! Now shall they be appreciated, now shall they receive the proudest prize of all—the approbation of the World.

THE END

CONTENTS.

SONNETS TO FRIENDS.

THE GOLDSMITH OF PADUA.

THE LATHAM PRIZE POEMS.